SURVIVAL!

TRAIN WRECK
KANSAS, 1892

K. DUEY AND K. A. BALE

ALADDIN PAPERBACKS

FOR THE WOMEN WHO TAUGHT US THE MEANING OF COURAGE:

ERMA L. KOSANOVICH
KATHERINE B. BALE
MARY E. PEERY

First Aladdin Paperbacks edition January 1999

Copyright © 1999 by Kathleen Duey and Karen A. Bale

Aladdin Paperbacks
An imprint of Simon & Schuster
Children's Publishing Division
1230 Avenue of the Americas
New York, NY 10020

Library of Congress Cataloging-in-Publication Data
Duey, Kathleen.
Train wreck, Kansas, 1892 / K. Duey and K.A. Bale.
— 1st Aladdin Paperbacks ed.
p.   cm. — (Survival! ; #8)
Summary: In 1892 Max and Jodi, young employees of a traveling circus, find their
lives endangered when their train wrecks in a storm.
ISBN 0-689-82543-9 (pbk.)
[1. Railroad accidents—Fiction. 2. Railroads—Fiction. 3. Circus—Fiction.
4. Survival—Fiction. 5. Elephants—Fiction.]
I. Bale, Karen A. II. Title. III. Series: Duey, Kathleen. Survival! ; bk. 8.
PZ7.D8694Tr   1999
[Fic]—dc21   98-41011
CIP   AC

CHAPTER ONE

The wide doors stood open on the elephants' boxcar. Old Mom was anxious, and Maximo fit his bull hook over his forearm, freeing his hands to rub her leathery skin. The train master was walking down the line, shouting orders. Max tried to remember where they were. Beloit, he was pretty sure. Beloit, Kansas.

Today was Sunday, so there would be no performance. A day off. Max tried to recall the last Sunday he had spent anywhere but aboard a moving train. He couldn't.

The sun was almost up. The gray light silhouetted Hickory's sloping back and enormous ears. He was chained nearest the door so he could be unloaded first. Hickory didn't like the train, and he could sometimes be hard to handle if he got impatient enough. Next to him, Donner, Front, and Big Girl were half turned to look outside. Trilby and Norma were still sleepy, their massive heads low and their tails and trunks motionless.

With the bull hook swinging from his arm, Max rested his hand lightly on Old Mom's shoulder. "I'll give you a scrubbing today," he promised her. "I'll make sure you get a good bath." She reached toward him with her trunk, fluttering a breath over his face. She was swaying in her chains now. Hickory began trumpeting, a sound that ricocheted deafeningly off the boxcar steel. Max put his fingers in his ears, his eyes moving from one huge animal to the next, alert to any sign that the elephants were about to act up. If they did, he would be expected to try to calm them.

The idea of being in a boxcar with seven unruly elephants scared Max, but only a little. Mr. Cooper would be watching him, and Max was determined to prove himself. Mr. Cooper never showed any sign of fear, not even when he was working the big cats.

Hickory finally stopped his noise, subsiding into a raised-trunk whuffling sound. Through the frame of the open doors, Max saw the cookhouse wagon roll past. He could hear the clanging of the crossover plates as they were shoved into place. It wouldn't be long before the wagons at the front of the train were hitched, one by one, to the pullover teams, and unloaded.

With her trunk, Old Mom nudged the bull hook to one side, then pushed gently at Max's jacket pockets. She knew he had an apple for her. She also knew she wouldn't get it until the train was half unloaded. She loved apples and she knew that standing still and being patient would be the price of this one.

Mr. Grayson looked in. "All right here?"

Max straightened. "Hickory's uneasy, but I think he's okay."

Mr. Grayson nodded curtly. "I'll bring up the rear. You walk up front with Old Mom."

Max nodded, but Mr. Grayson was already gone, working his way down the line of boxcars. Max talked to Old Mom in a low, comforting voice. He saw the ticket wagon go by, then the office wagon. The first tableau wagon, with its fanciful carvings of angels and cherubs, rumbled past, drawn by a hitch of six Percherons. The heavily muscled horses walked steadily, their heads high. They would be surprised when they were unhitched at the lot instead of being plumed and garlanded for a parade.

Old Mom lifted her trunk and touched Max's cheek, then his shoulder. He no longer flinched when she was affectionate, but he could never forget how strong she really was. He had seen her kill a pig once. The squealing animal had escaped from a farmer's wagon, then run past the elephants, blundering into Old Mom's leg. Startled, she had lifted her trunk only once, the motion so swift that Max had not had time to react in the instant it had taken for the two hundred pound pig to crash to its knees, its neck broken. The farmer had been furious, but as upset as he was, he had kept his distance from Old Mom while she sidled and trumpeted.

The metallic clanking of the crossover plates came closer, and Max watched two more tableau wagons roll past. The second one was his favorite. It depicted the story of the Sleeping Beauty.

Jodi Jamison had played the part when Max had first seen the Hamilton-Shaw Railroad Circus in Hermosillo a year ago, but another girl did it now. Mr. Cooper had put Jodi up on Old Mom to add a little more flair to the parades. Jodi's training as an equilibrist made it easy for her to stand on the howdah platform, balancing against Old Mom's swaying gait. With Jodi's long hair and her satin cape billowing out behind her, it was a striking parade stance—the crowds always cheered.

Old Mom had not liked the cape at first, but she had gotten used to it. She liked Jodi, too. Max reached up to stroke Old Mom's wrinkled skin, rubbing gently just above her trunk, where she liked it best.

When the next three tableau wagons had gone by, Max reached into his pocket. Old Mom waited until he held out the apple on his palm, then whisked it into her mouth without touching his hand with her trunk. She crunched the fruit contentedly, and Max was sorry he didn't have a second apple to give her—but he knew Mr. Cooper was right. Even when there were extra apples, it'd be wrong to give her more.

Mr. Cooper said that if Old Mom came to expect extras, she would be upset when she didn't get them—and the other elephants were often affected by her moods. She was the eldest. All the others respected her.

"Ready in there, Maximo?"

"Yes," Max shouted back, automatically gripping his bull hook and lifting it from his arm. Mr. Cooper's voice had startled him, and he realized he had relaxed into daydreaming. It was the kind of mistake that killed animal trainers. He bent to unhook Old Mom's chains as four animal attendants scrambled into the car. Talking quietly and moving slowly, they spread out, freeing the elephants in the order that they would step down the ramp that was being locked into place by roustabouts on the ground. Mr. Grayson waited outside. Max saw him glance at his watch, then pocket it as the elephants started to move.

Hickory went first, and the whole boxcar

trembled with his weight as he went down the metal incline, his chains rattling. Old Mom followed him without any guidance at all. Max walked beside her, keeping close to her massive head as she stepped onto the railroad siding.

Hickory's attendant slowed him, and Old Mom went around, taking her rightful place at the head of the line as the other elephants emerged into the grayish light of dawn. Skulking through the train yard, a scruffy white dog started barking when it saw the elephants. Hickory trumpeted. He hated dogs. Max kept himself alert, light on his feet.

"Tail up!" Mr. Cooper shouted, popping the long black whip he always carried. It was a sound as sharp and quick as gunfire, and the elephants shambled into place, each one reaching with its trunk to grasp the tail of the animal in front of it.

"Mr Grayson?" Mr. Cooper called. "Move them out, please."

Mr. Grayson gestured at Max. Max nodded and touched the back of Old Mom's heel with his bull hook as he spoke the command. She started forward. Up ahead, the long line of tableau wagons moved slowly, turning up a dirt road in the distance. Max hoped the lot was at least a mile away. The elephants needed to stretch their legs before they were tethered again. He glanced back at Mr. Grayson, who walked beside Trilby, the calm old female that brought up the rear.

Walking fast to keep up with Old Mom's long stride, Max heard high-pitched giggles of excitement as he led the elephants past the last few flatcars. Looking up to his left, he saw a line of towner kids, perched on the flat roof of a grain shed. They were pointing and staring, poking each other.

Max glanced back. Mr. Cooper was busy with the cat cages, now. The new Bengal was throwing itself against the bars again. Max could hear Mr. Cooper calling for more help with the team. The horses would not approach the cage wagon or submit to being harnessed until the big cat stopped roaring.

"Hey!"

Max turned to see one of the towner boys

sliding to the ground. "Don't come too close," Max shouted back, then glanced at Mr. Grayson to see him nodding his approval.

"Is this okay?" the boy asked, trotting to catch up, then walking parallel with the elephants. He was grinning, his sunburned face alive with amazement.

"Sure," Max said, then looked at Mr. Grayson, who nodded again. Max knew that letting people get a look at the animals early sometimes meant a bigger turnout for the parade. "Haven't you ever seen an elephant before?" Max called to the boy.

The boy nodded, still grinning. "Twice." His eyes were lit, fastened on Old Mom.

"If you come all the way to the lot, I'll see if you can feed Old Mom. She loves peanuts."

"*Old Mom?* That's what you call her?"

Old Mom lifted her trunk as she heard her name spoken by the stranger. Maximo held his bull hook ready just in case. "Don't come any closer."

"I won't," the boy said quickly. Then he fell silent for a few steps. "You're so lucky," he said, looking up. "I wish my family was with the circus."

There was so much longing in the boy's voice that Max smiled. "But I don't have a family. It's just me."

The boy's eyes widened. "Then how did you—"

Max squared his shoulders. "Mr. Cooper hired me. He says I can learn to be a trainer if I work hard enough."

"I'd give anything to do that," the boy said quietly.

Max wondered if it was true. It had been for him. He had never even gone back to the mission to get his clothes. He half turned and saw Hickory sidling along at an angle, trying to get a look at something.

"Tail up!" Max shouted sternly, and Hickory came back into line. Mr. Grayson gave Max another approving nod.

The boy whistled between his teeth. "You just say that and they obey you?"

Max glanced at him and saw a look of pure admiration on his face. "Mr. Cooper trained them. That's what I want to do. And cats, too— lions and tigers."

The boy was shaking his head. "You mean with the whip and the chair and everything? There was a man in last year's circus who put his head right inside a tiger's mouth."

"Mr. Cooper does even better than that," Max told the boy. Up ahead, he saw the last of the tableau wagons turning up the dirt road.

As they got closer, the boy's grin faded. "I'd better stop here. Mama said to stay at the train yard."

Max shrugged, glancing back along the line of elephants. "You coming to the big top show tomorrow?"

The boy nodded and grinned again. "Pa says we can go for the evening show." He looked off toward the grain shed, and Max knew he was wondering if his friends had been watching him all this time. "Nice meeting you," the boy said as he stopped, then stood watching wistfully as the line of elephants lumbered past him.

"Step left," Max said quietly, straightening his shoulders, even though he knew full well that Old Mom was smart enough to follow the tableau wagons all the way to the lot by herself.

The closer they got to the field where the circus was setting up, the more onlookers they passed. Whole families had come out to watch. Their wagons lined the edge of the cornfield that bordered the road.

"Hold your horses!" Max kept shouting, keeping to the center of the road. "Elephants coming through!"

Up ahead, the heavy wagons were rumbling around another turn. Hickory trumpeted once more as Old Mom rounded the corner, his huge flat feet raising puffs of dust with every step. Max glanced back. Mr. Grayson was coming up alongside Hickory to steady him.

When Hickory trumpeted a second time, Max turned to see the huge bull swing out of line, his trunk raised over his head. It was only then that Max noticed the white dog again. It must have been slinking along after them all this time. Now it began to bark again, a shrill, sharp sound. Hickory started toward it, and Mr. Grayson raised his bull hook. Max stopped Old Mom, bringing the whole line to a halt. Then he ran to help, his bull hook swinging from his arm.

CHAPTER TWO

"Jodi? We should get up!"

Jodi opened her eyes and saw Aunt Sophia leaning down from the top bunk. Her dark hair was loose, and her eyelids were puffy, but her sunny smile made her pretty. Jodi watched her swing down in one graceful movement, landing on her feet. "Hard to believe it's Sunday, isn't it?" She yawned.

Jodi nodded. "Papa said we could go into town later and get a real supper at a restaurant."

Aunt Sophia stretched, then placed one foot on the edge of her bunk and leaned forward, touching her forehead to her knee. She switched legs and did it again, then smiled. "Dominic and I would love to join you. It's been more than a month since we've eaten anywhere but the cook tent before a show or the pie car once we're loaded up and rolling again." She sighed, and for a moment she looked so much like Mama that Jodi felt her heart ache.

"Maybe we could go on a picnic," Jodi said, fighting the tangled emotions that came every time she thought about her mother. Jodi knew that Mama was up by now, that she had hoisted herself from bed into her invalid's chair and rolled it out onto the porch to watch the Iowa sunrise. The housekeeper Papa had hired had complained at first, but Mama insisted on keeping circus time.

"You going to practice this morning?" Aunt Sophia asked, and there was a studied casualness in her voice that set Jodi's teeth on edge.

"I don't know," she answered. "Maybe."

Aunt Sophia nodded hesitantly. She and Uncle Dominic and Papa had all told her the same thing: She was going to lose her nerve if she didn't push herself.

There was a loud knock on the metal door

that separated their compartment from the central corridor. "Time to rise!" Mrs. Ting sang out. She had taken it upon herself to make sure everyone got up on time. She always knocked on all six doors in the coach. Jodi knew it made the Hannovers angry, but everyone else seemed to like the reminder.

"We're up," Jodi shouted, and heard the footsteps continue on. A second later, Gert Trammon's voice boomed out, then Mrs. Gellerian's.

Jodi crumpled her blankets and held them to her chest, wishing she could sleep a few more hours. Usually on Sundays, they could. When they were making a long jump between towns, the train just kept rolling and no one cared who slept in. Not even Mrs. Ting.

"It's going to be sunny, it looks like," Sophia said, lifting one of the window shades.

Jodi sat up and reached for her clothes.

"I'll get Dom to string up a rigging on the lot," Aunt Sophia said. "That way, if you feel like it later on—"

"Thank you," Jodi said, cutting her short,

wishing that this Sunday would just go on forever, that she would never have to try to face
the high wire again.

"Stay where you are," Mr. Grayson com-
manded.

Max stumbled to a stop, then repositioned
himself beside Old Mom. The white dog darted
beneath a high-sided hay wagon pulled by a
team of farm horses. Hickory stepped forward,
trumpeting. The white dog was barking fren-
ziedly, running stiff-legged toward Hickory,
then leaping back under the wagon when the
huge bull lowered his tusks.

Max stared, holding his breath as Mr.
Grayson prodded Hickory with his bull hook.
A family sat in the hay wagon, transfixed. There
were two little girls staring up at Hickory, their
necks craned back as though they were staring
at the moon.

Max patted Old Mom's shoulder, giving her
the command to stay, then keeping up a stream
of reassuring chatter.

The elephants were all watching Hickory

and the dog, their huge heads turned, their ears flared out. A half circle of onlookers was forming, and Max swept an arc in the air with one hand. "Stay back," he screamed at them. Whether they heard him above Hickory's trumpeting, or just understood the gesture, they retreated a few steps.

Abruptly, Hickory fell silent, and Max could hear the dog barking again. "Get out," Mr. Grayson was shouting at the family in the wagon. "Get away from the dog!"

The little girls seemed to understand him first. They sprang up. One leaped to the ground and ran. The other grabbed her mother's sleeve and pulled her forward. Then their father seemed to come to his senses. He jumped out of the wagon, hauling his wife after him, then turned back to grab his hesitant daughter, swinging her over the slatted wagon rails. All four of them scuttled backward, their wide eyes on Hickory.

The big bull elephant was swaying back and forth now, and the heavy chains attached to his leg cuffs rattled. Max saw Mr. Grayson lift his bull hook high, shaking it in Hickory's face as he scolded the elephant sternly. Max started forward, then saw Mr. Grayson motioning him back. "Stay with the others!" he shouted.

Just then, the dog came out from beneath the wagon, snarling, the hair on its back raised into an angry ridge. From somewhere off to Max's right, someone threw a rock. It might have been meant for the dog, but whoever threw it hit Hickory in the side of the face, close to the big bull's eye. The dog chose that instant to advance another few stiff-legged steps, and Hickory forgot everything but his desire to kill it.

"Get back!" Max heard himself shouting at Mr. Grayson. But it was too late. The maddened elephant charged. He grazed Mr. Grayson with his shoulder and threw him aside like a rag doll. The bull hook fell, and Hickory stepped on it, shattering the heavy oak. Max heard a woman scream.

Lifting the edge of the wagon with his tusks, Hickory flipped it over. The harness dragged the horses backward, and they whinnied in terror as Hickory shoved at the overturned hay wagon, each push sliding it fifteen or twenty feet farther into the cornfield. The horses were dragged along with it, plunging and fighting. The dog danced backward, barking furiously.

Then, without warning, the dog darted out into the open, and Hickory whirled on his hind legs, moving with astonishing speed. Max walked the line, cajoling, pleading with Old Mom and the others to stand calm. Then he turned to watch helplessly as Hickory caught the dog in his trunk, lifting it high, squeezing the life out of it before he threw it down with enough force to break every bone in its body.

"Max! Move the others up!"

The voice was stern and sudden, blending with the pounding of hoofbeats. Max looked up to see Mr. Cooper hauling his horse to a stop, swinging off to hit the ground running.

"Get back," he ordered the crowd. "We'll handle this. Please, just clear off."

There was a calmness in Mr. Cooper's voice that seemed to bring everyone back to reason. A murmur went up from the crowd as people moved back.

"That's it, give us room to work, folks," Mr. Cooper shouted again. He strode toward Hickory, handing the reins of his horse to a man as he passed. Mr. Grayson was struggling to his feet, and Max heard Mr. Cooper say something to him in a low voice, but he couldn't understand it—or Mr. Grayson's answer.

Mr. Cooper walked around one of the parked wagons, then came back onto the road facing Hickory. He stood very quietly as the big bull reached out to turn the dead dog over with his trunk. For a full minute, Hickory pushed the dog's body around in the dust.

The whole crowd was silent now. Max saw the farmer advance carefully, pulling a knife from his locket to cut the traces of his own harness. He led the horses out of the way, and Hickory did not seem to notice.

"The show will pay for your wagon and any injuries, sir," Mr. Grayson called in a pinched voice. Max saw him limping back into the cornfield to talk with the farmer. Animal attendants were running up the road. Mr. Cooper slowed them to a walk with one imperious gesture.

"Bring me your hook, Max," he said in a low voice.

Max pressed his hand against Old Mom's chest to remind her to stay put, then he stepped away from the line. "Tail up and stay," he said in a curt tone as he walked down the line of elephants, intending to take a circuitous path around Hickory. The big bull had laid the dog aside now and had raised his head. The dark fury had left his eyes, and his trunk hung low once more.

"Come all the way around the wagons," Mr. Cooper instructed. Max veered into an even wider curve that took him through the crowd and out into the cornfield. He turned back, following the example Mr. Cooper had set, walking straight toward Hickory.

"Pass it to me from there," Mr. Cooper said when Max was a few steps away. Max stopped and extended the hook. Mr. Cooper took it and turned to face Hickory. "Go back the same way and stand with Old Mom," he said over his shoulder. "She likes you. Tell Smith to see if Grayson needs a doctor and ask him to have somebody get that damn dog out of the way as soon as I manage to move Hickory. I just hope it was a stray."

Max walked back into the cornfield and worked his way through the crowd once more. By the time he got to Old Mom, Mr. Grayson was sitting on the gate of a baggage wagon that had been rolled forward. He looked flushed and weary.

Smith and the other animal attendants had closed ranks around the elephants. They were all talking in low voices. As Max approached, he overheard Mr. Smith sending someone back to the train for more bull hooks and a bag of apples. Max repeated everything Mr. Cooper had told him to. Mr. Smith nodded and motioned for the attendant at Old Mom's head to step away, and Max took his place. The elephants had closed ranks. Trilby had moved up to take Donner's tail in her trunk.

Standing beside Old Mom once more, Max watched as Mr. Cooper faced Hickory down. He never even uncoiled the whip tied to his belt. All he did was talk. His voice was low and terse, like a loving parent scolding a destructive child. Hickory lowered his head, shaking his tusks. Then he swung around without warning and moved toward Donner.

"Give him room!" Mr. Cooper shouted.

Max watched the attendants react quickly, pushing Trilby back in time for Hickory to step into his accustomed place behind Donner.

"We hope you all will join us in the big top tomorrow," Mr. Cooper shouted. "We will try to make the show at least as exciting as all this has been." The crowd laughed a little. Mr. Cooper made a show of withdrawing his wallet and handing money to the farmer as a group of attendants righted the wagon.

"And," Mr. Cooper said dramatically, raising his voice so that all could hear, "this gentleman and his family will attend as my personal guests." A smattering of applause broke out as Mr. Cooper gestured to the owner of the hay wagon. "Reserved seats, of course," Mr. Cooper added, and the applause swelled.

"Move them along now, boy," someone hissed close to Max's ear, and he jumped, startled to see Mr. Grayson standing beside him. For a second, Max didn't react, and Mr. Grayson leaned closer, wincing, one hand pressed against his ribs. *"Move them!"*

"Step forward," Max said to Old Mom, then straightened to cue her by leading off. She followed, as docile as any lamb, the rest of the elephants going along behind her. For the first time, Max realized that dozens of wagons and performers had been waiting for Hickory to be subdued. When he glanced back at Mr. Cooper, the trainer was surrounded by excited townspeople, and the body of the white dog was nowhere to be seen.

CHAPTER THREE

Jodi woke to the sound of the canvas men shouting as they loaded their tools and set out for the lot. A half hour later, she heard the faint ringing of the sixteen-pound hammers on the tent stakes. By midmorning, the big top was up, and her father insisted she go with everyone to check the setup.

Everything seemed fine, and after a few minutes Aunt Sophia and Uncle Dominic went back to the pad room to finish dressing for the parade. Jodi went to stand beside her tightwire rig, then glanced back at her father. He was still fiddling with the tension on the high wire, testing it with his own weight, then climbing back down to adjust it again.

The big top was almost empty. The morning sun shining through the canvas overhead made everything look gilded, beautiful. A few rigmen were checking the guy wires that held the sixty-foot center poles. At the far end, in the third ring, Jodi saw someone practicing a pratfall. As she watched, Viktor Kulik, the Auguste clown, stood up and brushed himself off, then took two steps and fell again, his long, thin legs sticking straight up into the air.

Jodi smiled. The crowds loved Viktor. So did the circus people. He was known for kindheartedness. Many performers had borrowed money from him to ease some problem at home or to buy new equipment or costumes. Just as many had found him at their bedside when sickness or injury kept them from working. Viktor had gone through two years of medical training back in Russia before the circus had captured his heart.

"I am going up now," Papa said, and Jodi glanced at him as he started up the ladder. Then she turned resolutely away and strode to the tightwire. She swung herself up and went through her routine, ending just as Papa called out. "Jodi!"

Reluctantly, she looked up at him. He was halfway across the wire, working with the balancing pole held low in his hands. That meant he was practicing for the carry. At the end of their act, he and Uncle Dominic fastened poles to their shoulders, connecting them like two men carrying a stretcher. Aunt Sophia balanced in a chair set on the poles. It was the same chair Jodi's mother had fallen from the year before.

Jodi hated the trick. She couldn't stand to watch it. As he practiced, Papa's face was a mask of calm concentration, and Jodi envied him. Somehow, he had managed to stop remembering the screams from the audience as Mama had fallen, the terrible blue-ash color of her lips, the way the towner doctor had shaken his head.

Papa kept saying Jodi could learn to concentrate again, but she wasn't so sure. She wanted to, more than anything. She had always loved walking the wire, had absorbed applause like the earth soaked in rain. But now? How could she forget, even for an instant, that Mama would never be able to walk another step as long as she lived?

Jodi forced herself to keep watching Papa as he slid one foot, then the other along the steel wire. She imagined the poles that would connect him and Uncle Dom a few hours from now, and pictured Aunt Sophia in the chair. Aunt Sophia would be smiling, looking for all the world like a woman doing something she enjoyed. The audience would not hear her whispering prayers or see the half-moons of perspiration on her velvet costume.

"Come up, Jodi," Papa called. He was standing on the tiny platform at this end of the wire.

She shook her head, then nodded. Then she shook it again. "Perhaps tomorrow, Papa."

"You must keep trying, Jodi," he called down to her. "If you try, you can put the fear behind you."

Jodi looked aside. "You promised—"

"I promised I would help you," Papa said. "And I am trying to. Your mother—"

Jodi lifted her chin. "Mama said it was up to me."

"Of course it is. No one is saying different."

Jodi stared up at her father. The finger-thin steel cable that stretched from this platform to one exactly like it nearly thirty feet away was almost invisible from where she stood. For the evening show, it would be, except for the occasional glint reflecting the coal oil lights.

"Come up the ladder and just stand with me," Papa cajoled.

Jodi started to shake her head, then didn't. There was no harm in going up the ladder. But then she imagined herself walking the wire and felt a cool sweat break out on her forehead. But maybe if she stood with him, he would leave her alone for a few days at least. Perhaps, by the next time he asked, she would be ready. "All right," she said, pulling in a deep breath.

The ladder was made of thin steel tubing strung over rope. Jodi climbed steadily until she was halfway up, then slowed, fighting the feeling of nausea that had plagued her since Mama's accident.

"You see?" Papa said as she reached the top and stood clinging to the rungs, her face at the level of his feet. "Now, just come up here and—"

"I can't," Jodi whispered, already starting to feel the strange sensation that something was trying to pull her off the ladder, was drawing her away from its safety.

"Give me your hand, Jodi." Papa's voice was steady. "Come up on the platform with me."

Jodi hesitated, then raised her right hand. Papa gripped her wrist and lifted her straight up. From long habit she bent her knees as he swung her upward, then straightened them gracefully and landed catlike beside him.

"See? You're all right."

Jodi clung to her father's arm, staring at the wire. It was so far to the other platform—she wasn't sure she could ever walk it again.

"Here," Papa said. Before she could react, he was lifting a balance pole from the rack and raising it over her head. He lowered it slowly, his hands spaced widely enough that she could easily take it from him.

"I don't want to," Jodi said, her heart pounding.

"One step," Papa said. "Or two."

Jodi let him place the pole in her hands. Then he moved back, giving her room to center herself. Jodi hefted the pole. It was twenty pounds—the weight she had been using for two years, ten pounds less than anyone else. It felt familiar, almost comforting in her hands. The bar had been freshly resined. Her father always kept it ready for her.

"Don't think too long," Papa said. "You can do this, Jodi. If you want to, you can."

Jodi nodded without turning to look at him. He was right, and she knew it. But she had been on the high wire only twice since Mama's fall. Both times, she had made it across, then climbed down the ladder, shaking and nauseous.

"It will be simple," Papa encouraged her. "No tricks, no dancing or back walk, nothing fancy. Just a stroll."

Jodi swallowed, her throat tight. She had walked a high wire for the first time when she was seven. She had fallen a few times into a net. It had never hurt more than a few days while the bruises healed. She looked down.

"Jodi, you know the net is there. You don't need to look."

Jodi nodded. And how much good had the

net done Mama? She had fallen awkwardly, landing headfirst, then bouncing out to hit the ground. Jodi winced, imagining the pain her mother had felt.

"Think only of the wire," her father said gently. "Just take a step or two."

Jodi took another deep breath and set her shoulders. She aligned the toe of her slipper on the wire, then hesitated again. "Papa, I—"

"You will feel much better when you have won out over the fear," he answered her.

She nodded, but she still couldn't make herself take the first step.

"Jodi!" His voice was a little sharp now. "The big top is empty. It's all yours. Remember your mother's courage and strength. You have both."

Jodi swallowed and lifted her chin. She slid her right foot onto the wire. Holding the weighted pole low enough to make each change in her balance less critical, she brought her left foot out and around and placed it on the wire, careful to center the cable between her first and second toes. She bent her knees and then straightened them, feeling the resilience of the cable and the slow bounce of the flexible pole.

"Good girl," she heard her father murmur.

Jodi slid her right foot forward again, the cable familiar and unfamiliar all at once.

"Focus on the platform," Papa whispered.

Jodi lifted her eyes from the wire to the platform at the far end. This was no different from the tightwire she performed on nearly every day. It was just higher. Measuring her breath, sliding one foot forward, then the other, she slowly started across the terrifying stretch of steel cable.

The platform seemed to inch toward Jodi, and by the time she set her balance pole into the bracket and stepped off, she was almost crying from relief. Her father's applause startled her, and she turned to look at him. "Bravo!" he shouted, punching the air, beaming at her. "I am proud of you!"

Jodi smiled. She felt trembly and sick, but she didn't want to spoil Papa's excitement. She measured her breathing again, letting the slow rhythm steady her. Then, before she had time to even think about it, she ducked beneath the balance pole and pirouetted to face the wire again.

Going back seemed faster. The balance pole kept her firmly upright, and when Papa reached out to take it from her hands, she nearly burst into tears.

"Nothing has changed except you are not afraid now," Papa said. "You are better at thirteen than most will be at thirty."

Jodi sniffled, smiling.

"You will perform tonight? Just the tricks you have been doing on the tightwire, nothing more."

Jodi felt her stomach tighten. "Not yet, Papa. I—"

"Not this afternoon's show," he said quickly. "This afternoon you can build your confidence by staying on the low wire. But tonight—"

"I can't," Jodi said.

He gripped her shoulders. "Of course you can. Why not? The fear is conquered."

"I can't," Jodi repeated. She started down the ladder, closing her eyes to shut out the sight of the ground so far below. She counted the ladder rungs until she knew she was nearly down, then opened her eyes again. Viktor was standing a little way off, watching her. As soon as he knew she had noticed him, he applauded as Papa had done.

"I am going to practice a little," she called to Papa. He was smiling at her, his face shining with pride. Jodi forced herself to smile back at him, then headed for the tightwire. Refusing to look at her father, she stretched, forcing herself to relax. Then she mounted the low wire from below, swinging up and placing her resined slippers perfectly.

Pulling in a slow breath, Jodi began her routine. She arched her back and, widening her arms for balance, danced a few steps forward. Here, five feet above the ground, she could do anything she had ever done. She could hear her father and Viktor talking, but she ignored them, concentrating on her own movements until their voices faded and her focus was complete. She felt wonderful, buoyant. Maybe she would be able to perform by evening. Jodi felt her stomach tighten and willed herself to focus.

CHAPTER FOUR

Max's eyes were watering from the dust and the acrid steam that rose from the calliope. His high, stiff collar itched. The parade had been staged at one end of the lot, and the wagons and costumed performers stood in a loose line that curved from the entrance road down the incline past the menagerie tent, all the way to the other side of the big top. The elephants were next to last. Behind them, there was only the hitch of eight Percherons that pulled the heavy steam-operated calliope.

Old Mom was standing calmly as usual. Jodi was already perched on the platform atop the elephant's back, wearing a flowing Arabian costume. Max had tried talking to her, but she seemed preoccupied or upset, and he had decided it was best to leave her alone with her thoughts.

Max looked back down the line. Every elephant carried a rider in costume—three men and four girls. There were extra animal attendants working the parade today. No one wanted any more trouble.

Max scanned the line, checking each elephant for signs of distress or uneasiness. Mr. Cooper had asked Mr. Grayson to ride Hickory for the parade and the grand entrance. Max had caught a glimpse of the assistant trainer's blue-black bruises in the pad room when he was changing into his costume. Max wondered if Mr. Cooper knew how badly Mr. Grayson had been hurt. It might not have mattered. The important thing to Mr. Cooper was that Hickory not be allowed to cause any more trouble.

"Move up!" The shout came down the line, and Max knew that the parade had finally begun. He stepped a little to one side to watch the owner's carriage and the brigade of trumpeters as they started off in their gaudy red costumes. The driver of the number one band-wagon waited for almost a full minute, then touched his whip to the backs of the wheelers in the twenty-four horse hitch. The instant the pair of Percherons hitched closest to the wagon began to lean into their collars, he raised the whip and popped it sharply over the backs of the pairs in front.

"Can you see the crowd?" Max asked Jodi.

She straightened up and shaded her eyes. "It looks pretty thick, at least at this end of the route."

Max nodded. "That's good." He waited for Jodi to say something more, but she didn't. People said she had been a lot friendlier the season before—before her mother had gotten hurt.

"Move up!" The shout was relayed once more.

The sideshow wagon that carried Fred Harris, Elizabeth Hedge, Mildred Walker, and Franz Miller rounded the corner and started down the street. Max loved the banners affixed to the bright green wagon, announcing its passengers The Siberian Albino Giant, Elephant

Woman, Gordia the Mysterious Knot Lady, and Flamo, the Fire-eater.

Max waited for the forward movement to work its way down the line. The horses were fidgeting this morning, even the staid Percherons hitched to the cage wagons.

In front of Max, the line moved. He gave the clown ahead of him time to stop his miniature team of Shetland ponies and climb down off his seat to check the tiny South American monkeys that rode in the scaled-down cage wagon.

"Ready?" Max asked Jodi.

"Yes," she answered without looking down at him.

Max touched Old Mom with the bull hook, and she stepped forward. The others came along in good order. Max glanced back to see the calliope driver urge his team into motion. The lumbering machine was silent now, except for the hissing of steam as its engine heated up. Max pitied the driver and the calliope player who would manipulate the keyboard and make the deafening whistle-music from his perch swathed in steam and black smoke. Max saw two roustabouts crossing the lot with bags of coal for the boiler.

The band launched into "The Washington Post March" by John Philip Sousa. Max liked all of the Marine Corps Bandmaster's music. Mr. Hamberg, the bandleader, had told him that nearly every circus in the United States used some of his pieces.

"Move up!"

Max stepped to one side again. The cage wagons were rolling out now. He could see the Bengal pacing as its wagon turned onto the road. At least it wasn't lashing out through the bars yet. If it started to, Mr. Cooper intended to put the sideboards up. The crowds loved to see the big cats roar—but it wasn't worth the risk of someone getting hurt. There were always a few kids who refused to stay back, no matter what anyone told them.

Max hoped that the freckle-faced boy would be somewhere in the crowd. He probably had already bragged to his friends about talking to a real animal trainer. The shout came down the line, and Max moved the elephants up again, careful not to crowd the pony wagon.

"They've got Viktor up on Cleopatra's

Palace," Jodi said suddenly. "It has to be him. There isn't another man that tall or that thin in the whole show."

Max strained to see. "Why? I thought he was always with the second group of clowns." He glanced up at Jodi, envious of her high perch. She was still staring at the tableau wagons as they rumbled out onto the street.

"He can do anything. Last year he did three or four roles and clowned—and drove a chariot in the race. He can juggle, too. And walk a wire. Papa says he could have been any kind of equilibrist if he'd wanted to."

Max looked up at her. Her eyes were wistful, sad. He wanted to tell her that he knew the awful story about her mother. He'd heard a lot of stories—about animal trainers being mauled and aerialists missing a catch and falling. For the first few weeks, people had tried to talk him into going home—especially Mr. Cooper.

"I want to have my own animal act," he said when he realized that Jodi was still looking down at him. She nodded vaguely and didn't answer.

"Move up!"

They were getting close to the front, and Max watched the elephants carefully. Hickory's tail was switching, but he stayed in line and Mr. Grayson didn't seem to be having any trouble with him. Max waited as the Wild West riders whipped their horses up and made them rear and squeal. Their blank pistols flashing fire, they whooped and shouted, heading down the street. Every circus seemed to have them now, people said. And everyone was looking for a woman sharpshooter to compete with Mr. William Cody's famous Annie Oakley.

In the next group, clowns were dressed as policemen. Max could hear the children at the head of the parade route laughing as the clowns pretended to arrest a grinning boy. The laughter swelled as they spun him around, catching him beneath the arms and carrying him to the brightly painted paddy wagon with bars on the windows. The boy would get free tickets, Max knew. So would the other children the clowns accosted along the way.

The third group of souvenir sellers went

next, giving the crowd another chance to buy. The hawkers began their noisy chants the moment they appeared in the street, then spread out, walking alongside the clown, working the crowd.

The prancing ponies that drew the tiny wagon of monkeys rolled forward. The clown sat straight, mimicking a high-class carriage driver, holding the reins at chest level, his nose pointed at an upward angle.

Jodi stood up, gripping the gilded rope attached to the platform for balance.

"Ready?" Max asked.

She smiled at him. "Yes."

Cheers greeted the elephants as Max signaled Old Mom and led them forward. He glanced up at Jodi. Her head was high, and her parade smile was fixed on her lips. She lifted one hand from the rope and began to wave at the onlookers. Max glanced back to see the other riders do the same.

As they turned down the street, Max walked tall and proud. He loved the parades more than almost anything else about working for the circus.

The bright red coat he wore almost shone in the midday sun, and the gold braid that decorated the shoulders swung with his stride. Behind the elephants the calliope hissed and chugged into life. The shrill, whistling tune began—a sound that could be heard two miles away.

Max knew—and everyone in the circus knew—that he was walking with the lead elephant because Old Mom was the calmest animal of all. She probably could have led the string of huge animals trailing behind her without any kind of human guidance. The real assistant trainer was Mr. Grayson, riding second-to-last on Hickory. But the crowd didn't know that, and Max always found himself intoxicated by the gasps and exclamations that rose from the people lining the street.

There was a good turnout. Adjacent to the lot, along the first hundred yards or so, families had drawn their wagons up along the roadside and sat watching the parade form up. Where the sidewalks began, they stood shoulder to shoulder.

Max scanned the faces for the freckled boy

where the crowd was thinnest, then gave up. Hundreds of people stood beneath the awnings of the business district. Glancing up at Jodi, Max saw her forced smile and wondered if she knew how lucky she was. It was terrible that her mother had been hurt, but Jodi had been born into the best kind of life there was. And she was a very good wire-walker, Mr. Cooper had said. She certainly looked graceful as she performed. It was like magic to Max—he could barely do somersaults on flat ground, much less on a steel cable.

Max looked backward every few seconds to make sure there was no trouble in the line of elephants. Mr. Grayson caught his eye and nodded approvingly. Max paced Old Mom, keeping a good distance between the elephants and the little pony cart ahead of them. Jodi and the other riders kept up their waving and smiling as though each face in the crowd were someone they were happy to meet.

Max kept looking back at Hickory and Mr. Grayson. The big elephant seemed calm enough, in spite of the cacophony of the calliope so close behind. None of the animals liked the high-pitched steam whistles, but the elephants seemed to tolerate it better than many of the others. Max glimpsed people covering their ears as the calliope passed them. Behind the bellowing steam-organ, the crowd had closed in, following the parade.

The parade stalled once, and Mr. Grayson signaled Max to put Old Mom through a few of her simplest tricks. Soaking up the applause, Max had Old Mom lift one front leg, then the other, walking in a slow half-time rhythm that she performed in the Grand Entry every evening. Then he stopped her and fed her peanuts, opening his hand flat so that people could see the delicate movements of her trunk.

Max stepped back a few feet and shouted to the crowd. "Even our elephants think this is the greatest railroad circus on tour this season, don't they?"

At a subtle signal from Max, Old Mom nodded her huge head, ears flapping.

"And people who come to see the performance are assured of being entertained in a manner befitting royalty."

Again, Max touched Old Mom's side near her wrinkled flank. She nodded, an enormous, exaggerated movement of her head. Just then, the parade began to move again, and Max bent forward at the waist, bowing, then gestured toward Old Mom so that the crowd clapped even longer.

"Join us at the big top," Max shouted as he tapped Old Mom into motion again. "The performance will amaze and delight you!"

Max glanced at Jodi and saw a teasing grin on her face. "You sound like a sideshow talker," she said loudly enough to be heard over the calliope.

Max felt himself blushing. "Mr. Cooper said to play it up."

"He's right. People love a show," Jodi answered, starting to wave and smile as Old Mom stepped forward again.

"Papa wants me to walk the high wire tonight," Jodi said after a moment.

Max turned, not sure he had heard her

correctly over the noise of the crowd and the steam whistle. "Tonight?"

She nodded, and he saw the shadowed look come into her eyes again.

"You'll be great," he shouted as the crowd began to cheer the group of clowns ahead of them. He glanced back at Hickory and Mr. Grayson, then at Jodi's face again. She grinned her thanks for the compliment, and he envied her for a moment.

It would be years before anyone asked him to perform. But he was determined. Someday, he would be like May Wirth or Buffalo Bill, with fans by the thousands and newspapermen waiting for him to step down from his private railroad car. He would train his animals to do things that no one else had ever been able to. He looked sidelong up at Jodi. She was still waving, but her real grin had faded behind her parade smile, and her eyes were shadowed again.

★ ★ ★

The afternoon show had gone well enough, and Jodi was grateful. All her tricks had been executed smoothly, and Papa had made a big show of complimenting her. She knew he meant well, but she could not seem to stop dreading the evening performance.

The wind had kicked up in the early evening, and the canvas of the tents billowed, then sank in an irregular rhythm. The boss canvas man had his whole crew watching for tears or loosened stakes. They had been pacing the perimeter of the stable top when Jodi had gone to look for Max. He had been a few minutes late lining up for the evening performance's Grand Entry. All the animals were a little restless with the smell of a coming storm in the air.

Walking back in the wind, following the line of elephants toward the big top, Jodi fought with her veils and her wide skirt. She saw the cook wagon breaking down and the calliope wagon heading back toward the train yard. Everyone would be hurrying to reload if the weather turned.

As the Hannover sisters on their milk-white horses galloped through the open flaps of the huge tent, Jodi could hear the crowd roar to life. Papa and Aunt Sophia and her uncle all rode in a chariot in the first part of the Grand Entry—so they were lined up way ahead of her. She was glad to be away from her father for a little while, she admitted to herself. He had been trying to encourage her all day long, and it had only made her more afraid.

Performers were chatting all around Jodi as they waited. She could hear Fred Harris talking about his children—all five of them home with his wife in Wisconsin. The Gellerians, the aerialists, went on endlessly about the farm they were going to buy come winter. Everyone was commenting about how the chicken at supper had been better than usual. Max caught her eye, and she walked toward him.

He was standing attentively beside Old Mom. "Do you want to get up now?"

Jodi hesitated. It was a little early, and the elephant platform was uncomfortable. Still, she nodded. Up on Old Mom, no one would expect her to talk at all.

"Thank you, Max," she said politely.

"Down," Max said firmly. Old Mom lowered

herself onto her knees. Jodi climbed up. Clinging to the handholds as the elephant lurched from one side to the other standing up again, Jodi waited until the big animal had steadied beneath her. Only then did she let go long enough to arrange the cloth of her skirts and straighten her veils. When the cue came, Max asked if she was ready, and Jodi nodded.

The Grand Entry was spectacular, but Jodi had little to do beyond sitting still and smiling. The choreography of dozens of animals was the responsibility of the trainers and attendants. The cheers and applause of the audience meant nothing to Jodi. She had not earned it. She allowed herself a single glance at the high wire rigging in the center of the tent. The wire seemed closer from atop Old Mom. Jodi forced herself to stare at the crowd, refusing to look back up.

CHAPTER FIVE

The wind was rising. Max walked the elephant line once more. Every water bucket was full, every chain was correctly fastened. The animals were calm, finishing up their evening meal of hay and vegetables. All but Donner and Old Mom would soon be taken back to the rail yard and loaded for the night. Old Mom still had a part to play in the finale. Mr. Grayson would put her through an old routine that always pleased the crowds, lying down while she stepped over him. Donner would be harnessed and used to pull down the center pole and help load the canvas when the show was over.

Joe and four other animal men were rolling

dice for pennies, waiting for the elephants to finish their supper.

"We won't tell if you want to go in the big top for a while," Joe offered, looking up at Max.

Max nodded eagerly. "I'd love to go watch the——"

"Big cats," Joe finished for him. "Just be sure you get back before it's time to walk the bulls back down to the train."

"I will," Max promised. He stopped to push a flake of Old Mom's hay closer to her, watching the flecks of green scatter in the wind. Then he hurried toward the big top.

The front entrance was off-limits to circus employees, but that wouldn't matter. Max made his way through the sparse crowd around the sideshow tent, then angled toward the big top. All the canvas was in motion, billowing, then collapsing when the wind hesitated. Max continued around to the back. There was no one else in sight. He lifted a flap of canvas and rolled beneath it, coming up under the last row of the blues. Here, in the cheap seats, there was always a spot or two where someone could squeeze in unnoticed. Max maneuvered his way through the close-packed crowd and finally slid onto the end of one of the narrow plank benches.

The beacon lights shone like a false summer in the center ring. There, in a steel-barred cage less than twenty feet across, Mr. Cooper was cracking his whip, his brilliant silver costume sparkling. The Bengal was going through its paces, and Max stared, transfixed.

Mr. Cooper had been training the magnificent cat for less than six months. It was spectacularly beautiful, stealing the show from the lions and leopards that sat on their stands, snarling.

Max watched Mr. Cooper working all these cats as often as he could. He knew that most of his education as an animal trainer would have to come from watching—very few performers were willing to take the time to teach.

The tiger loped around the perimeter of the cat cage, then, at the snapping of the whip, veered toward a hoop and leaped through it. The whip popped again and the cat whirled, loping back in the other direction. Overhead, the first spatters of rain hit the big top. The odor of wet canvas filled the air.

The crowd gasped as the running Bengal leaped through a second, smaller hoop that Mr. Cooper held out. The tiger sailed as lightly as any house cat, then landed and turned to face Mr. Cooper.

Max leaned forward, staring. This was not part of the act. The cat was supposed to continue its circular path, running once more around the big cage. Sitting tensely, Max watched Mr. Cooper face the tiger. He popped the long whip close to the animal's head, trying to turn it around and force it to go back to its stand as it had been taught. But the huge cat stood its ground, roaring. Max saw the attendants move closer, and he knew they were gripping their feeding forks, ready to leap forward to try to protect Mr. Cooper.

The big cat roared again, and Max held his breath. The audience had become restless. He could hear people shifting in their seats. None of them understood that a battle of wills was going on. If the three hundred pound cat attacked Mr. Cooper, the attendants would do what they could from outside the cage, but no one would open the door—not even if the tiger killed Mr. Cooper. The risk of the cat getting out was something no show owner would permit.

Max gasped with the crowd as the cat advanced a few steps, then stopped, dropping into a tense crouch. An instant later, it sprang. Mr. Cooper fired a blank from his pistol into the cat's face just as its huge paws struck him, its weight bearing him to the ground.

Max leaped to his feet and started toward the ring. He managed to step past the people sitting beside him and made his way into the aisle. People were standing up, getting out of their seats as they tried to get a better look. Max could see Mr. Cooper ducking away from the huge jaws, trying to roll himself beneath the tiger's chest where it couldn't reach him as easily.

As Max made his way through the throng, he kept catching glimpses of the horrible fight. Attendants were stabbing at the tiger, their sharp steel forks barely reaching the big cat. As it snarled, trying to fend them off, it shifted its weight back onto its haunches.

Max pushed his way past a group of boys who had crowded up against the rope that separated the audience from the arena. Mr. Cooper had rolled to one side and was struggling to his feet. Aided by the tines of the attendants' feeding forks, he backed the cat off, cracking his whip in a series of sharp explosions just inches from its face.

The Bengal, confused and subdued, sprang back onto its pedestal. Mr. Cooper turned and took a deep bow. The audience went wild. Max stumbled to a halt as the attendants moved away from the cage. The crowd was cheering now, a deafening sound that muted the resentful snarls of the cat.

Max watched closely as Mr. Cooper took his position between the pedestals again and went on with his act. Outside, Max heard the rain coming down harder. Mr. Cooper was hurt— Max just couldn't tell how badly.

Jodi stood on the high platform. Aunt Sophia and Uncle Dominic were on the opposite platform. Papa was on the wire now, waltzing to a lilting melody played by the band. He was so graceful, his movements fluid. He was in perfect time with the band, using the slack in the wire to put a spring in his steps. His posture was like a dancer's.

It was getting windier, and raindrops spattered the tent lightly, but none of the crowd was leaving. The music came to a stop as Papa dismounted on the far side. Aunt Sophia pretended to dance with him for a few seconds, her parasol lifted high in her right hand. Then she stepped onto the wire and began her routine.

The music changed. For Aunt Sophia, the band played a smoother piece, a melody that showed off her incredible balance and control. She walked the wire forward and backward, the parasol raised a little about the level of her shoulders. Jodi had never gotten good with a parasol—they were much harder to work with than the heavy balancing poles.

Aunt Sophia stood near the center of the wire and raised herself onto her toes like a ballerina. Slowly, she extended one leg behind her, leaning forward until her heel was higher than her head. She held the pose for a long time, the parasol moving constantly as she readjusted her balance. The crowd applauded.

Jodi felt her nerves tightening as Aunt Sophia traded her parasol for a balancing pole. Finally, her part of the act came to an end with her famous back somersault. Poised, she bent her knees, then sprang backward, turning in the air and landing lightly on the wire again. As they did at every performance, the audience was silent for an instant, then cheered.

Jodi bent to resin her slippers, then straightened. She waited for Aunt Sophia's last bow. Then she picked up her balancing pole and pulled in a deep breath. All Papa wanted her to do tonight was to walk the wire. If she was comfortable, he had said, she could step over her balancing pole and walk backward a few steps, nothing more. He just wanted her to perform, to increase her confidence.

The pole felt odd in Jodi's hands. She took a deep breath and timed her first step onto the wire with her exhalation. She slid one foot along, then the other. She kept her eyes on the far platform, using every bit of her training to keep from being distracted by the pounding of her heart.

Jodi was almost to the center of the wire when the whole tent flashed blue-white with lightning. An instant later, there was a ground-shaking crash of thunder. Jodi flinched and leaned to her left. Automatically, she lifted that end of her pole. The heavy weight corrected her balance, and she lowered her hands carefully, her heart hammering.

The big top was billowing in the storm, the canvas moving dizzyingly all around her. Without meaning to, she looked straight down, toward the net far below. By the time she realized she had made a terrible beginner's mistake, it was too late. She was fighting a losing battle for her balance, leaning too far to one side, unable to correct. Somehow, she managed to remember to loosen her grip on the pole. Her mother had clung to hers. It had hung up on the wire for a second or two, sliding so far that Mama had lurched sideways, very nearly missing the net. Jodi heard her father shout something, but couldn't understand his words, even though the audience was silent now.

As she fell, Jodi shoved the pole away and managed to turn onto her back, but she hit the net hard and bounced upward halfway to the wire. Terrified that she was going to miss the net this time, she clawed at the air and landed gracelessly, one leg twisted beneath herself, only to rebound once more at an angle. She heard a groan go through the crowd as she plunged downward a third time.

Flailing her arms, Jodi managed to catch at the edge of the net and hang on, dangling over the edge. She heard her father shout as the rough rope cut into her hands. She hung on grimly until the net steadied, then she finally let go and dropped to the ground. A roar of relieved cheers and applause burst from the crowd. Flat-footed, standing stiffly on the ground, Jodi's eyes filled with tears. Her father was coming down the ladder as Aunt Sophia walked back onto the wire and the band struck up another tune.

Papa reached Jodi's side. "Are you all right?"

She looked at him, tears streaming down her face. Her shoulder hurt and her leg ached and her hands were bleeding, but she knew what her father meant, so she nodded.

Papa lifted his shoulders and head into the proud stance of a performer, facing the crowd. Jodi tried to imitate him as he leaned forward, pulling her with him, bowing. A second later, he walked backward and Jodi went with him, bowing again as he pulled her out of the arena, into the privacy of the rainy night.

"Are you sure you aren't hurt?"

Jodi shrugged. "Not bad, Papa, but I am so sorry."

He held her tightly for a few seconds. "You have learned that you can fall and come out all right, yes?" he said into her ear. Then he stepped away from her, and she nodded so that he could go do what he had to do—finish the act. "Yes, Papa."

"I will see you in the pie car if not before. Stay with Sophia. You did very well, Jodi. You kept your wits."

"Yes, Papa," Jodi repeated. As he ducked back

through the canvas, she heard the crowd cheer. Then she turned and started off through the spattering rain, heading toward the long tent where the performers would be changing costumes for the next spectacle act.

CHAPTER SIX

Max kept glancing at the canvas sides of the pad room. He felt a little sick. The wind slapped at the tent and blew scattered rills of rain through every hole and slit in the cloth. Mr. Cooper's arm had inch-deep slashes where the tiger's claws had pierced his costume.

Viktor appeared with a bucket of clear water and clean rags. Max winced as the Auguste clown, his jaw set, poured the water into the ragged wounds. Mr. Cooper's face was as white as clean sheets, his brow studded with sweat.

"We will let the wounds bleed a while longer," Viktor said when Max stepped forward to help. "The cat's claws are poisonous."

Max watched the blood seeping up out of the wounds, then had to look away again as Viktor ladled more water into the jagged cuts. A group of attendants hovered near the entrance of the tent.

"I'll be fine. Get back to work," Mr. Cooper said between his teeth. "All of you. This storm is likely to get worse."

The men began to leave the tent. Max stepped back to get out of the way, but he couldn't seem to take his eyes off Mr. Cooper's arm. He felt almost dizzy.

"Go on, boy," Mr. Cooper said tightly. "The animals are in an uproar."

"Are you going to be all right, sir?" Max blurted out.

"I think so," Mr. Cooper told him, then drew in a quick breath as Viktor flushed the bloody wounds again. "I might have to fight a fever for a few days."

"Bandages now," Viktor said, setting down the bucket.

Mr. Cooper nodded, then looked back at Max. "See to it that no one is rough with that cat until I can get down to the menagerie, will you, Max?"

Max nodded, still reluctant to leave. He knew he wasn't doing Mr. Cooper any good just standing and staring, but . . .

"I'll take care of him, Max," Viktor said quietly, wrapping the first layer of clean cloth around Mr. Cooper's arm.

Max took one step backward, then spun around and left. A gust of wind spattered him with rain as he started toward the menagerie tent. He could hear shouting as he got closer.

Ducking through the door flaps, Max saw that most of the cages were already gone. Lightning flashed. On a normal night, the menagerie would have been completely broken down by now, the tent and poles stacked and waiting for the canvas wagon. Tonight, the storm made everything harder. Men were still pushing the cage wagons to the back entrance where pull-up teams stood waiting.

The Bengal's cage stood alone on one side of the huge tent, and there was a knot of men around it. A heavyset man was dragging his feeding fork along the bars. The racket was agitating the cat. It was pacing, lashing its tail and snarling.

As Max watched, the man turned and he recognized him. Mr. Greeley was a sour-tempered man. Max watched him stick his feeding fork through the bars, jabbing at the tiger.

"Mr. Cooper says to leave the cat alone!" Max shouted, coming forward.

Mr. Greeley pulled the fork free and swung around to face him. "Mr. Cooper can give his own orders, boy."

"He asked me to make sure," Max answered, coming a little closer.

The man spat. "I take orders from Mr. Cooper, not from you."

Max took another step forward. "I heard you. I'm telling you what Mr. Cooper said."

"You don't listen, do you, boy?" Mr. Greeley took a step toward Max.

"Leave him be," Mr. Smith put in quietly.

Mr. Greeley rounded on him. "Mind your own business, old man."

"It's all right, Mr. Smith," Max said. He stood

his ground. "You've made the cat more dangerous, hurting him like that."

"You're no animal trainer," Mr. Greeley
scoffed. "The boys have told me about you,
wandering into that Mexican train yard. You're
just a scruffy little orphan."

Max refused to respond to the insults. "Mr.
Cooper asked me to make sure no one was
rough with the cat." He forced himself to take
another step, staring into the man's face. Mr.
Greeley turned and jabbed the sharpened tines
through the bars again. Max grabbed at the
handle. Mr. Greeley shoved him. Max staggered
backward, then, in two quick steps, he dodged
around the heavyset man and positioned himself in front of the cage.

Mr. Greeley lifted the fork. "Get out of my way."

Max shook his head. The other men moved
back.

"Let it go, Greeley," Mr. Smith said.

"Is there a problem, Mr. Greeley?"

Startled, Max saw Mr. Cooper standing just
inside the tent flaps. The bandages were already
stained with blood.

"I'm just teasing the boy," Mr. Greeley answered.

Max squared his shoulders. "He was taunting the Bengal, Mr. Cooper. I told him what you said."

Mr. Cooper nodded, coming forward. "Mr. Greeley, I don't want you around my animals anymore. I suspect you've been stirring up the Bengal when no one was around. If so, you caused this." Mr. Cooper gestured at his bandages. "You'd better ask Mr. Shaw to switch you to canvas man or rigger or something else."

Max saw Mr. Greeley narrow his eyes. "You can't do—"

"Speak with Mr. Shaw," Mr. Cooper cut him off, then turned to Max as Mr. Greeley walked away. "Thank you, son," Mr. Cooper said quietly. "Will you help keep an eye on things if I get laid up? Mr. Grayson can't be everywhere at once. If you see anything like this, I want to know."

Max nodded. The sheen of sweat was still on Mr. Cooper's forehead. He turned to go out, then stopped at the tent flap. "The menagerie should have been down an hour ago. Get started, all of you. I'll explain the delay to the canvas boss."

Jodi shivered as she closed her trunk and fastened the strap buckles. Her hair was wet. The wind snaked under the canvas into the crowded pad room. Lightning flashed. Jodi buttoned the top button of her coat.

"The train yard is going to be muddy," Aunt Sophia said.

Several women chimed in with groans. "Pity the razorbacks and the roustabouts," Gert said. "They'll be in those filthy bunks with the windows closed tight tonight."

Another round of groans rose in agreement. Jodi sat still on top of her trunk, waiting for Aunt Sophia. She felt numb. No one had said a word to her about what had happened, not even Papa. They probably all thought that the less she dwelled upon it, the better. But their silence made her feel isolated, as if she had awakened from a nightmare and couldn't tell anyone about it.

As the friendly chatter went on, Jodi stood up and went to lift the canvas to peek outside. The lot was nearly empty. The cookhouse and calliope were gone, of course, along with the parade wagons and everything else that wouldn't be needed until the next town. But usually the sideshow tent would still be up. Not tonight. The rain was chasing everyone home early. The big top was emptied, and only a few straggling towners hung about, hoping to see some of the animals, probably. They were out of luck, Jodi knew. The menagerie tent was being knocked down now. All the cage wagons were on their way back to the train.

"Jodi?" She jumped, startled. Aunt Sophia was standing right behind her. "Is your trunk ready?"

Jodi nodded, and Aunt Sophia gestured. "Let's go, then."

Aunt Sophia lifted the hem of her dress and led the way. There was a line of wagons leaving the lot. The new electric generator still ran, rain streaking through the work lights. Jodi could hear shouts and the sounds of men straining to lift wet canvas.

Uncle Dominic and Papa had already gone to the train with the other men. The wagoner helped Aunt Sophia up onto a bench, then turned to Jodi. The rain had made the steps slick. Jodi ducked under the canopy and sat next to Aunt Sophia, sliding over when Gert and her daughter got on. They were both stout, as muscled as men from their years of practice with the heavy juggling pins.

Jodi watched the women come up the wagon steps one by one. Some of them had known her most of her life. Some of them she barely knew. Still, no one said a word about what had happened, and she knew they expected her to lick her own wounds. She was too upset to talk about anything else, so she was silent. It made her feel invisible.

The wagon driver took it slow going over the dirt roads. Everything was a sea of mud. The train looked small and dismal in the darkness, its windows glowing with yellowish light. The men's coaches were closer to the front of the train than the women's coaches, but all had their side doors open wide. Beside every open coach door was a lantern. The sharp smell of coal oil permeated the damp air.

Jodi followed Aunt Sophia up the metal steps and into their coach. The narrow vestibule had even narrower corridors leading off in both directions. In their quarters, Aunt Sophia pulled off her coat and hung it up.

Jodi's bunk was neatly made. Her locker door was closed, and she knew exactly where everything inside it was placed. Her costume trunk was the same way. Not a single thing was ever out of place. Neatness was something her mother had taught her by making sure she had gotten a peek or two into the roustabout cars. Nomads learned to pack well, or they ended up living with clutter that rapidly became filth.

"Come with me to the pie car?" Aunt Sophia was toweling her hair.

Jodi nodded. She didn't really want to see Papa now, but she dreaded getting into bed and being alone with her own thoughts even more.

Aunt Sophia opened the door, and Jodi followed her up the narrow corridor, then stepped across the steel plates that formed a bridge between their coach and the next women's car. The corridor was crowded. Six cars up they saw the end of the line of women waiting to get into the pie car. They joined it, moving up every few seconds, their backs pressed against the wall to let women carrying food get past them.

The line moved fast as usual, winding through the tables where people sat chatting or playing cards. At the counter, Jodi asked for apple pie and milk. Sophia got a sandwich. Jodi was turning to leave when she saw Papa near the front of the men's line. He smiled, and she worked her way to the rear of the car and waited for him. Aunt Sophia gave her a wave and left.

Once he had gone through the line, Papa came back around the crowded tables and stood close to Jodi, smiling down at her. "You will be fine tomorrow. You should go up for the afternoon show, though. Don't give yourself time to worry over this."

Jodi looked up at him, wishing their hands were not full of plates and silverware, wishing he would just hug her. Mama would have.

He winked. "The audience loves a fall when no one is hurt. Mr. Shaw said he heard people talking about it going out."

Jodi blinked and fought to keep from crying, from throwing her food, from running away from him. The pie car was suddenly so confining that she could barely breathe.

"See you in the morning," Papa said.

"All right," she managed.

He ruffled her hair, then walked away. Jodi watched him. He would never talk to her about how scared she was. He had nursed a broken toe for half the previous season, but he had never once mentioned it. Circus people kept their troubles to themselves.

Jodi started back toward her berth. Her eyes were flooded with tears, and she wanted more than anything to tell someone how she felt. She wanted to see her mother. Jodi instantly felt guilty. Knowing she had fallen would worry her mother.

Preoccupied with her grim thoughts, Jodi very nearly ran into Mrs. Ting's daughter, then came close to spilling her milk when someone bumped her going past. Tears were rolling down her cheeks now, but no one noticed—or they pretended not to. Jodi kept on down the narrow corridor, passing through each car quickly, alone with her fear.

CHAPTER SEVEN

The engine whistle blew at about midnight. Five minutes later, the shouts for all aboard rang out. Then the whistle blew again, and the doors were closed. As the train eased forward, it was still raining lightly.

Max had spread his bedroll beneath the number one bandwagon. It was a coveted spot, held by the men who had been with the circus the longest. Mr. Smith had walked fifteen flatcars back to the supply wagon where Max usually rolled out his blankets—and had asked him to move up. Twenty men had greeted Max as he had followed Mr. Smith back to the front of the flatcars.

"Ain't no one really likes Greeley all that

much," Mr. Smith had explained as Max fixed his bed. "Word spreads fast."

As the train built up speed and headed into a long curve, Max settled in. Lying on his back, he let the rhythm of the rails rock him from side to side. He would never understand the men who seemed to prefer to sleep inside the crowded coaches. He had heard men say they were afraid of falling off the flatcars, but that was silly.

Max yawned and stretched. Unless someone was foolish enough to stand up and try to walk when the train was jerking its way over a section of rough track, there was no danger. He had slept inside the first four nights of his stay with the circus, then never again. The sleeping coaches were airless and smelly. The bunks were three high, and most of the men bathed only once a week, on Sundays.

"Mr. Cooper is a good man," Mr. Smith said, scattering Max's thoughts. He was still sitting up on his blankets, his arms wrapped around his knees, staring off into the darkness.

"He's been more than fair to me," Max agreed, sitting up again.

Mr. Smith laughed. "Brave, too. You couldn't get me in that cat cage for anything." He shook his head.

Max stared up at the ink-dark sky. "That's the only place in the world I want to be." He turned his head to look at Mr. Smith.

The old man was silent for a few seconds. Then he shrugged. "People think I'm crazy to live like this at all. But the circus has been a better home for me than my own ever was."

Max started to ask if Mr. Smith was an orphan, then he stopped himself. Jodi had been the one to explain to him that no one in the circus liked questions. "Good house tonight," he said instead.

"Indeed it was," Mr. Smith agreed. "The blues were so full, I thought we were going to have to raise them to fit all those people inside. I think nearly everyone in that town wanted something to take their minds off the storm."

"It's much drier here than where I was," Max said. "I appreciate it, Mr. Smith." A wind-driven shower of rain burst over Max, dampening his face and blankets.

"Speaking of dry," a voice said from behind Mr. Smith.

All the men laughed, and Max joined them. He felt good. The train was still speeding up. They must be hitting the open country between towns. Max wished he could see it. When they traveled in the daytime, he loved to watch the green valleys and cornfields rush past the train. He liked crossing rivers and gorges, too. The trestles, with their hundreds of braced timbers, fascinated him. They had crossed one early in the season that had been almost two hundred feet above a deep chasm. The river below had looked like a silver ribbon.

"We'll roll right through this storm," Mr. Smith said. He got under his blankets. "I can sleep through wet if it doesn't get too windy."

His friends made sounds of agreement.

"Rain is better than stink, any night," Mr. Smith added after a few seconds, and they all laughed again.

Max leaned back, staring up at the undercarriage of the enormous wagon. The shadowy struts and crosspieces were nearly three feet above his head. And the wagon was almost as wide as the flatcar. This was the best place on the whole train to sleep.

"Shame about that little girl falling off the wire," the man farthest from Max said suddenly.

Max half sat, facing the unfamiliar voice in the darkness. "What girl?"

"That little blonde, Joany, I think her name is."

"Jodi," Max corrected him. "Is she hurt? How did she—"

"There was a bolt of lightning that distracted her, I think. She fell pretty far to one side, but she caught the edge and made it down all right. Her father walked her off."

Max felt sorry for Jodi.

"Got a big show tomorrow," Mr. Smith said. "I'm turning in."

"Thanks, Mr. Smith," Max managed to say. "This is a lot drier than being under that little supply wagon."

"You earned it, sonny," Mr. Smith answered. "Good night." Then there was no sound except for the endless heavy rolling of the steel wheels on the tracks.

Max pulled his shoes off, but he then lay back down, fully awake. His thoughts kept going back and forth between Bengal and Jodi's fall. Mr. Cooper always had said that the circus was dangerous, that every day brought a chance to die. Max hadn't really listened to him even though he had seen a lot of performers get hurt in the year he had been with the circus. After a few minutes of wondering, he figured out why he felt so uneasy now. Today, two people he liked and cared about had come close to getting killed.

Max rolled onto his side and closed his eyes, but sleep would not come. Usually the rocking of the flatcar lulled his thoughts into silence, but tonight was different. Images of Mr. Cooper's bloody wounds kept rising in Max's mind. The idea of getting hurt like that someday scared him, but not nearly as much as the idea of Mr. Cooper dying. What would happen if he did?

Max knew he might be able to stay on with the circus, but maybe not, too. He was much younger than most of the animal attendants. Max saw a glimmer of starlight and realized he had opened his eyes. Was the storm clearing? An instant later the stars winked out, and he knew that clouds were still covering much of the sky.

A few minutes later, a rumble of thunder and a fresh downpour made Max curl up to avoid the rain that blew under the big wagon. Mr. Smith mumbled something in his sleep that Max couldn't understand, but the old man did not waken—even when the rumbling became crashes of thunder and the sky was lit with crackling lightning.

The storm finally began to subside, and Max still lay awake, the smell of the rain-soaked fields heavy in the air as the train hurtled through the night. The lightning came further and further apart. In the blue-white light, Max saw Mr. Smith, relaxed and still soundly asleep.

Restless, Max sat up. The next bolt of lightning was reflected in an expanse of water and Max squinted, trying to see ahead, but the crackling light failed, and he could not. The next flash lit up the countryside again, and this time Max saw that the train was approaching a lake, or a flooded river. He caught just a glimpse of the long trestle it would have to cross.

There was a pause between the stark-white flashes of lightning, but when the next one came, Max could see along the curving line of the train. They were coming onto the trestle, and it was a high one.

As the lightning died, Max heard the unearthly squealing of tortured metal. The first jolt that hit the flatcar knocked Max over. He rolled, grabbing at his blankets, then at the riveted steel of the flatcar. He caught frantically at a wheel spoke and tried to hang on as he slid out from under the bandwagon.

The second jolt hit Max like an invisible iron fist. He was torn from the wagon wheel and thrown into the air. He curled up around his terror, grabbing his knees with his hands. Time seemed to stand still, and he thought he would fall forever. He had an instant to wonder if he would die tonight. Then cold water smashed into him from below, stinging his skin and cracking his jaw shut against his knees.

★ ★ ★

Jodi awoke, clawing at the darkness. A second later she smashed into the berth wall, and something heavy pinned her right leg. She struggled to understand the nightmare she was having, then, a second later, knew it was not a dream.

A shrill screaming sound assaulted her ears, and whatever had pinned her leg fell away. She heard Aunt Sophia shout once, then the high-pitched shriek deafened her again. Something struck her in the middle of her back, and she had to fight to breathe as the floor seemed to rise at an impossible angle. She slid down it, unable to think, to react. Beneath her bare feet was a smooth, cool surface.

"Jodi!"

This time Aunt Sophia's shout was loud enough to hear, but Jodi could not answer. Her breathing was ragged, and the ache between her shoulder blades was still almost more than she could stand. The floor angled a second time, and the shrieking of twisting metal rose until there was nothing left in the world except the awful sound. Jodi fell backward in the darkness and struck her head on something hard and sharp. Then, abruptly, the world was still and silent again.

Jodi found herself lying facedown. The surface beneath her hands was bulging, uneven. She lifted her head. "Aunt Sophia?"

There was no answer. Jodi rolled onto her side. Something flat grated beneath her leg, and she blinked, shaking her head. It slid like ice along the bulging metal, and she suddenly understood. The windows had broken. "Aunt Sophia?"

There was still no answer, but for the first time, Jodi heard other voices. There was a thin, wailing scream somewhere close by, and Jodi hoped that Mrs. Ting and her daughter were all right. There was a heavy slamming sound from next door, and Jodi heard Gert shouting, then heavy dragging sounds in the corridor.

Jodi pushed herself up and sat, shaking, the pain in her back still sharp. The train had wrecked. It had happened to other circuses, she knew. Now it had happened to them.

Jodi managed to get to her feet. "Aunt Sophia? Aunt Sophia, where are you?" The quavering voice that Jodi heard barely sounded like her own.

A pounding on their door made Jodi jump, but whoever it was didn't call out, or tarry. She heard more thumping and dragging in the corridor.

Without warning, a flash of lightning arched overhead. Jodi found herself looking straight up through the broken windows and she began to understand what had happened. The coach was on its side. She stood still, shivering as rain began to fall again, coming through the shattered windows above her head. She looked down, thinking about the Hannovers and the Gellerians. Their windows would be resting against the ground.

Jodi held still in the darkness, praying for another bolt of lightning. When it came, she saw her berth standing vertically, Aunt Sophia's beside it. Jodi's trunk was overturned, and she saw a crumpled shape near the far wall that she knew was her aunt. Then the sky went dark again.

"Oh, no," Jodi whispered as she took a single step toward her aunt. Beneath her foot, a slab of glass slid, grating on the metal. Jodi froze. She had to get her shoes.

Breathing lightly, listening for voices close enough to call for help, Jodi waited for the sky to light up again. When the lightning came, she spotted her locker sticking up from the wall that had become her floor. She made her way slowly toward it, moving her bare feet through the shattered glass as though she were walking the wire, sliding first one foot forward a few inches, then the other.

The door on Jodi's locker was bent and hard to open, but she managed it. When a flash of lightning lit the jumbled wreck of her shelves and boxes, she spotted a pair of work trousers she sometimes wore for dirty chores and slid them on. Then she began at one end of the tangled mass of her belongings and sorted her way through them. Quick flashes of fading lightning did little to help her see.

She found one shoe quickly, then could not find the other for what seemed like an eternity. Once she had them both in her hands, she perched cautiously on the frame of her locker and pulled them on. She could hear women's voices all around her now, and muted thumps and bangs in the compartments on either side.

"Aunt Sophia?" she called, standing up. She walked across the broken glass cautiously, afraid she might slip on it and cut her hands if she fell. When she got close enough, she squatted, shards of glass grating beneath her shoes. Bending closer, Jodi could hear Aunt Sophia's slow, steady breathing. She was alive! Now, if only Papa and Uncle Dominic were all right.

Slowly, carefully, Jodi crossed the little room, walking on what had always been their wall. She felt her way to their berths and pulled her blankets free, holding them high to keep them out of the glass.

Working blindly, she laid out a crumpled pallet next to Aunt Sophia, then gently rolled her onto it. Aunt Sophia moaned a little, and Jodi rocked back on her heels, fighting tears. Maybe she was doing the wrong thing by moving her, but the glass . . .

"Jodi?" It was a barely audible whisper.

"Are you all right?" Aunt Sophia shifted on the blankets.

Jodi felt her wince. "What hurts? Is anything broken?" Jodi held her breath, waiting for the answer.

Aunt Sophia shifted again and winced a second time, a soft groan escaping her lips. "I'm so dizzy, I'm not sure I can walk. Is the train on fire?"

Jodi caught her breath. She hadn't even thought of that. She lifted her head. "I can't see anything. But the coach is on its side." She inhaled—there was no smell of smoke.

"Dominic," Aunt Sophia said, as if she were just remembering her husband. She struggled to sit up and cried out again.

"Just lie down," Jodi said, helping her ease herself back onto the blanket. Voices came through the broken windows again. Someone was shouting for help. Two or three people answered, then the shouts moved farther away.

"We have to find them," Aunt Sophia said. "Help me." She reached out, fumbling in the dark.

Jodi clasped Aunt Sophia's hands, bracing

herself as her aunt struggled to sit up. Jodi could hear her labored breathing. "Are you sure you should—"

"Get me outside, Jodi. Then go look for the men," Aunt Sophia interrupted.

Jodi half stood, trying to think. The windows were broken, but she couldn't reach them without standing on her berth, and even then, it'd be hard to pull herself upward. It would be impossible to lift Aunt Sophia without help. "Wait here and don't try to move yet," she said. Then she stumbled across the room, feeling for the door.

Crouching over it, Jodi fumbled for the handle. It seemed to work, but when she pulled on it, the door was stuck fast. Using both hands and bracing her feet, Jodi tried again. The wall had buckled slightly; the door was solidly jammed.

Jodi made her way back to their berths. She peeled off the top mattress and began to climb the wire frame. At the head of the bed, she felt a little jolt and realized the bolts in the wall had been loosened in the crash. Hurrying, she managed to get one leg over the framework, then the other. Breathing hard, she crouched in the dark for a second.

She looked upward through the empty window frames, trying to find a star, anything that would act as a reference and help her keep her balance. There was nothing except the flickering of distant lightning. Using the wall as a guide, she forced herself to stand. Then she freed her hands and reached upward. She could hear people screaming and the sound of terrified elephants trumpeting.

CHAPTER EIGHT

The first thing Max felt was the black water closing over his head. It was cold, and his whole body ached from the shock. He tried to breathe, even though his mind was screaming that he could not. Gagging, he panicked. He knew he had to get to the surface, and he began to swim desperately.

Seconds dragged past, and Max felt his heart hammering against his ribs. The water was deep. Or was he swimming sideways just beneath the surface? He changed directions, kicking hard. There was no way to tell which direction was up.

Suddenly, something soft brushed against his cheek, and he recoiled. He stopped swimming, his hands raised protectively in front of his face. As soon as he was not paddling, he felt himself rise in the water. Wrenching around to reorient himself, lungs burning, Max began to swim again.

The cold water slid beneath his clothes and billowed his shirt away from his back. It seemed endless. How deep could it possibly be? He had to breathe. He had to.

Seconds later, he broke the surface, coughing violently. He dragged in a desperate breath and then choked again. For a long time, he could do nothing more than breathe. The air felt light and strange as it rushed into his lungs. His coughing slowly subsided.

There were sounds in the darkness, terrible sounds. People were screaming and shouting, and the elephants were trumpeting frantically. Something tickled Max's wrist, and he jerked his arm upward to protect himself. Long, coarse hair caught on his fingers. Startled, he reached out to touch the body of a dead horse floating in the water.

Max splashed backward, his feet tangling with

the horse's legs. For an instant, he floundered. Using only his arms, he unwillingly towed the horse's body along with him for another few strokes, then managed to break loose.

Breathing hard, treading water, Max turned in a circle, his teeth chattering from fear and chill. How wide was the water? Maybe it'd be smarter to swim toward shore than try to get back to the trestle. But it was too dark to see the banks.

The trumpeting of the elephants carried in the night air, and Max hoped Old Mom was all right. On the heels of this thought came a few other names: Mr. Cooper, Mr. Grayson, Jodi, and Mr. Smith.

A flicker of lightning along the horizon gave Max a few seconds of murky light. He could see the trestle a hundred yards away, its heavy timbers broken and collapsed, the train angled in the middle like a broken spine. He still could not see the shoreline.

Not knowing what else to do, Max began to swim. The water was dark as night, and the sky overhead was black except for the occasional sparkle of distant lightning. It was so far away that it could dimly silhouette the collapsed tres-tle for only an instant before darkness closed back in. It was unnerving, swimming in the endless ink-black water. Max tried to stay calm, but the feeling that he was lost and would never reach safety was hard to fight. Then, sounds began to filter through the rasp of his own breathing.

He could hear water rushing somewhere up ahead. As he got closer, he could also hear voices. He stopped again, treading water, and listened. People were screaming and shouting. Max tried to make sense of the jumble of cries and pleas for help. A bolt of lightning split the sky, and he saw the wrecked train as clearly as in daylight for a split second.

Then, without warning, the water around Max began to rush past him in the dark. Something hit him in the shoulder, and he saw a crate of souvenir clowns go past. The water was full of debris. Before he could struggle against the sudden swift current, or even react, he was caught in it.

Max fought to keep his head above water,

dragging in one breath after another. It was all be could do. He bumped into the body of another horse. This one was a Percheron, its long white tail fanned out across the water.

Flailing to stay afloat, he hooked one arm through a tangle of heavy wire that had somehow wrapped itself around a shattered timber. He curled helplessly around it, pushed forward by the current. He doubled up, using his feet and hands in unison, but managed only to pull the wire free of the heavy wood. Freed of its float, the wire began to sink. On its way down, it caught at his trouser cuff and dragged him beneath the water.

For what seemed like an eternity, Max wrestled with the weight that was pulling him toward death. Jerking at his pants cuff, he finally tore the cloth and kicked hard, swimming backward away from the wire. Released from the terrible pull, he swam for the surface once more, feeling the rush of the water around him.

The current was so strong that when Max finally burst into the chill night air, he had no time to catch his breath. Gasping and coughing, he was hurtled along, fighting to keep his head above the glassy surface. The surging water had begun to roar up ahead, and a flash of lightning showed Max the trestle once more. This time he noticed enormous dark shapes bobbing in the water at the base of it. The lightning winked out, and thunder rolled.

As Max was swept closer to the trestle, lightning crackled overhead once more, and the clouds opened. Sheets of rain drilled at the black water. In the next flash of lightning, Max made out the huge arching wings carved into the number one bandwagon. It seemed impossible that he had been dozing peacefully beneath it a few minutes before.

The immense vehicle was slamming against the trestle. Beside it, three smaller wagons floated, and Max heard the heavy banging of tons of solid wood being shoved together as the current pinned them all against the undermined trestle.

Max began to swim hard, trying to work his way across the current quickly enough to avoid being washed into the wagons, but it was too late. A lightning flash brought the wagons into garish high relief as he was carried toward them. The carved cherubs and dragons seemed alive in the bluish light, and he had time to see the glitter of the gilded paint on the bandwagon before the relentless water slammed him into it.

Jodi pulled herself up, then shifted her weight to her forearms and wriggled through the empty window frame. She scrabbled across the buckled metal of the overturned coach, moving alongside the row of broken windows until she could get around them. Then she slid to the edge and looked down, waiting for a flash of lightning. Voices echoed in the dark, and she could hear someone sobbing. Chilly rain pelted against her face.

When the harsh white light came, Jodi could see the jutting undercarriage of the overturned railroad car, its wheels sticking straight out to the side. She was looking for a way to climb down when an odd spitting sound sorted itself out of the confusion around her. It took a few seconds for her to figure out what it was. The rain was hitting the wheels and hissing on the hot steel.

Shaking a little, grateful that she had hesitated long enough to avoid burning herself, Jodi started back across the coach, slipping on the slick metal. On the far side, she peered downward as lightning illuminated the earth. There was nothing in her way. Jodi leaped outward, jumping the eight feet to the ground. She landed, absorbing the shock with loose, bent knees as she had learned to do when she was five. She stumbled one step to the side, then righted herself, looking around as lightning crackled overhead once more.

People were walking in circles, alone and in pairs, swarming around the wreck like ants when their hill is kicked open. Horses galloped past, and she heard a dog whining. Voices rang out somewhere off toward the head of the train, then faded. The trumpeting of the elephants was constant. Jodi felt sorry for the animals. There was no way they could even begin to understand what had happened.

"Can someone help me?" Jodi called out.

Her voice was lost in the din. "I need help with my aunt!" she shouted again.

One man she did not recognize slowed and veered toward her, then seemed to change his mind and angled away, walking fast.

"Jodi! Is that you?"

She whirled around. "Uncle Dominic?"

"Over here!"

Jodi moved toward his voice in the darkness. "Is Papa all right?"

"I'm fine, Jodi," came Papa's voice from the dark, and Jodi felt her eyes fill with tears of relief.

"And Sophia?" Uncle Dominic called. "Is she with you?"

"She's still inside the coach," Jodi called over the sound of a horse whinnying. "I think she's all right, but she was unconscious at first and—"

"But she's all right?"

"I think so," Jodi repeated, then ran toward them, almost falling into her father's arms. He hugged her tightly, swaying to one side.

"My leg, Jodi—"

She stepped back. "You're hurt?"

"I can't walk very well, but I don't think the bones are broken."

"Is this your coach?" Uncle Dominic was walking past her.

Jodi nodded. "But watch out for the wheels. They're as hot as coals."

Uncle Dominic gestured. "Come with me." He bent one knee and laced his hands together.

Jodi felt Papa release her. "Go on. I need to sit down."

She stepped into her uncle's clasped hands and felt him straighten as he tossed her upward. She landed well enough, but the wet metal made her slip and she lurched to one side.

"For God's sake, be careful, Dominic," Papa called.

Dominic did not answer. He was walking around the coach, hesitating where the massive couplings joined their car and the one in front of it. Standing on the metal hitch, he leaped upward, both legs flying out to one side. He vaulted onto the coach and landed as clumsily as Jodi had. It took him less than a second to recover.

"This way," Jodi said, and led him past the broken windows to the last one in the row. "The berths are directly underneath," she explained, and he followed her back down into the coach.

"I am here, Sophia," Uncle Dominic called.

Aunt Sophia began to cry when she heard his voice. He crossed the room to kneel beside her, and Jodi heard them talking in low voices. "You already have a pallet made," Uncle Dominic said approvingly. "Let's get her outside."

There was a loud wrenching of metal as he forced open the corridor door. The other voices had stilled. Jodi hoped that everyone had made it outside.

Aunt Sophia was unconscious again when they went to get her. Jodi took the corners of the blanket by Aunt Sophia's feet. Uncle Dominic grasped the blankets near her shoulders. Awkwardly, they carried her across the room.

Lowering Aunt Sophia through the door was easier than Jodi had thought it would be. The corridor, turned on its side, was a long, low chute. Uncle Dominic led the way, crawling backward, pulling the blanket along with him. Jodi listened for voices behind the doors they were crawling across. She couldn't hear anyone now.

Uncle Dominic dragged the blankets past the last berth door. "Wait," he said, then clambered down to stand on the coupling. "Can you get a tight hold of the corners on your end? We can carry her best that way, I think."

"I can walk, Dom," Aunt Sophia said suddenly.

Uncle Dominic leaned over her. "You just rest."

"I can walk. Why are you carrying me like this, I . . ."

Aunt Sophia stopped in midsentence, and Jodi could hear her breathing slow and deepen, like someone who has fallen asleep.

"If you think you can't do this," Uncle Dominic said to Jodi, "tell me now."

Jodi was bunching the corners of the blanket, one in each hand. "I can do it."

"You come slow, now, and not before I tell you."

Jodi made a little sound so that he would know she had heard him. He lifted his end of the blankets, and Jodi felt Aunt Sophia slide a few inches farther. Jodi could imagine Uncle Dominic stepping straight out from the door, walking along the rounded coupling, holding the blanket edges tightly as he went. Everything depended on keeping the blanket more or less level. If Aunt Sophia's limp weight fell onto Uncle Dominic while he was still balanced on the coupling, he might drop her.

"Now, Jodi," Uncle Dominic said, breaking into her anxious thoughts. "You slide down. But you have to hold on to the blanket and keep it as low as you can. I'm going to step down to the ground as soon as you get your footing on the coupling."

Moving carefully, Jodi gripped the blanket corners, easing herself forward until she was sitting on the edge of the doorway, her feet dangling over the edge. Then she inched forward, relieved when her foot touched the coupling. As carefully as she had ever walked a tightwire, she shifted her balance point and her weight forward, keeping her two fistfuls of blanket at waist level.

"Stop there," Uncle Dominic said. She could feel the blanket swing like a hammock as he made it to the ground. A few seconds later, they were both down, walking as fast as they could around the side of the coach. It had stopped raining.

"Papa?" Jodi called.

"Here," he answered clearly. In the murky predawn darkness, they settled on a spot of level ground not far from the wreck, but far enough so that fire, if it started, wouldn't come too close. They were also well back from the steady stream of people milling along the line of twisted coaches.

Aunt Sophia was rolling from side to side, mumbling. Carefully, Jodi and Uncle Dominic eased the bottom blanket from beneath her, and Papa sat down heavily upon it. Lightning flashed, and a dry roll of thunder shook the ground. In the eye-blink of stunning white light, Jodi saw a deep gash in Aunt Sophia's scalp. The blankets around her face were soaked with blood.

"Oh, Lord," Uncle Dominic breathed. He looked around wildly. "I need to get her out of this chill. I need a doctor."

Papa was shifting sideways, making low, groaning sounds between his teeth. "Where's Viktor? His berth is up in front of ours a car or two, isn't it?"

"I'll find him," Uncle Dominic said, getting to his feet.

"Dominic," Aunt Sophia whispered. "Dom?"

He leaned close to hear what she was saying. Aunt Sophia reached up to touch his cheek.

"I'll go find Viktor," Jodi said, standing up, looking away from Aunt Sophia.

"You be careful," Papa said. "Find him and come straight back. And stay off that trestle. The water is undermining it now. The whole thing could collapse."

"I'll be back as quick as I can," Jodi promised. Lightning split the sky, and the dark splotch on Aunt Sophia's blankets blazed crimson in the sudden light. Jodi turned, stumbling into the darkness.

CHAPTER NINE

The force of the water was constant. Max was pinned against the side of the bandwagon, the current like a giant's hand, shoving him forward. As lightning lit the sky, he fought to free himself, but it was impossible. Looking up, he saw the timbers of the trestle above him, some jutting out, splintered.

Off to one side was a roaring of water, pouring beneath the broken trestle. How long before it washed away this section, too? Max wondered. He shoved backward once more and managed to drag himself a little ways along the side of the wagon before the water slammed him against it once more.

Shivering, closing his eyes against the bruising

pain, Max tried to figure out what to do. He could not fight the current, that much was clear. If he tried, he would exhaust himself and drown. Leaning back, he waited for more lightning. When it came, he looked up at the trestle once more, trying to gauge the distance between the timbers. Then, at the next flash, he twisted around and looked upstream, trying to see the shoreline. A stand of trees marked the end of the roiling water, but they were so far away. Too far. Thunder swelled, muting the sound of the water as it rose to a deafening crescendo.

The crackle of new lightning came before the sound had died. Max pulled himself up out of the water as far as he could, peering across the huge bandwagon. On the far side of its wide benches, another, smaller wagon was jammed between it and the first tier of timbers.

Max hunched forward, dragging himself over the gilded side of the bandwagon. The water seemed to clutch at him, and it took all of his strength to finally roll forward, falling across the third bench.

For a moment, he lay still, his breath heaving. He felt oddly heavy, as if his arms and legs were weighted and his muscles suddenly weak. Beneath him, the wagon vibrated with the force of the water flowing around and under it.

Max forced himself to lift his head, then sit up. For a bizarre instant, he imagined that he was riding in the parade, that somewhere in the darkness ahead were twenty Percherons, plumes nodding above their spangled harness. Then, a bolt of lightning showed him the stark reality again. For another few moments, he sat huddled on the bench, wishing he could stay there, feeling safe for the first time since the train had wrecked. But he wasn't safe, and he knew it. And there was only one way out.

Willing himself to stand, Max faced the trestle and waited for the storm to light the sky again. When it did, he shuddered, looking down at the ten or so feet that separated him from the lowest timbers. The small wagon rode the water at an angle, its hitch sticking upward, its rear wheels submerged. It was rising and falling violently.

Max recognized the wagon. It was usually used to haul feed, its wide flatbed made of thick, planked oak. It was half the length of the bandwagon he stood inside, and less than half its width and weight.

The next round of lightning was farther away and dimmer, but Max strained to see, to figure out some way to reach the trestle. As the thunder rumbled and faded, he moved closer to the front of the bandwagon and waited for more light.

The next streaks of lightning were off to the east and barely gave him enough light to fix his eyes on the moving bed of the wagon. He hesitated, losing his chance as the world was plunged back into darkness. The thunder was muted, distant. There was no way to know if the storm was over or not. He squinted up at the sky. There was just the faintest brightening in the east. It might be an hour before the sun rose.

Max steadied himself, and when the next pale lightning showed him the way, he forced himself to step over the side of the bandwagon. Terrified, he managed enough of a jump to land on the rough, slanting planks of the hay wagon, then fell, scrabbling for a handhold. He caught the back of the driver's bench with his right hand and took another step, steadying himself. He could feel the splintery surface of the oak planks grate at his bare feet. A low sound startled him. The rough planked wagon bed was grinding against the gilded side of the bandwagon.

Listening to the rush of the dark water all around him and praying for more lightning, Max could only hang on as the hay wagon was shoved upward by the water. It fell again, hitting the surface hard enough to loosen his grip. His feet slid out from under him, and he dragged himself forward, desperate to regain his stance. Finally, his arm hooked over the back of the driver's bench, he managed to jackknife, dragging his knees forward until he could kneel, then stand once more. A second later, the sky lit.

Frantic, Max twisted far enough to see the broken end of a timber jutting toward him, a narrow chasm of black water between it and the hay wagon. Then the sky went dark. He pulled in a deep, shuddering breath. His only chance was to be ready when the lightning came again.

Max let go with one hand and turned as far as he could, widening his stance. The wagon bed rose, then dropped hard, but he managed to keep his feet this time. Twice more he rode the wagon bed upward, then hung on as it fell back to the surface of the water. On the fourth rise, the sky lit up, white veins of lightning arching overhead.

In the glaring white light, Max forced himself to let go of his handhold and turn to face the broken timber fully. As the wagon bed lurched upward, he took one tentative step, then set himself and jumped, his arms wide, his heart pounding.

He landed, and the sky went dark. Thunder echoed and rolled as he bent forward to grip the sides of the timber with both hands. For a few seconds, he could only crouch there, reveling in the steadiness of the timber beneath his feet, grateful for its *stillness*. Then he began to climb.

Reaching upward, Max found the angled timbers that braced the next tier of the trestle. He clambered up onto them in the dark, then rested a moment in the V-shaped angle, shivering so hard that his teeth chattered. Then he stood and reached upward again.

He forced himself to keep his eyes focused on the next timber, the next angled resting point. The crudely sawn wood tore at his skin. For the first time that night, he was grateful for the darkness and dreaded the flashes of lightning that revealed the growing drop beneath him.

The pain in his hands and feet was numbed by the chilly air and his sodden clothing. Halfway up, it began to rain hard again. Digging his fingernails into the slick timbers, his mind as numb as his chilled feet, he kept climbing.

Finally standing on the highest tier of angled beams, the rain beating at his face, Max hesitated. Then he made himself put one arm over the edge of the railroad ties above. He heaved himself up, his elbows braced against the dark, oily wood. As his weight shifted forward, he swung one leg up and pushed himself away from the edge.

Lying flat on his back, breathing hard, Max closed his eyes against the rain. This far from the roaring water, he could hear voices again, and the trumpeting of the elephants. They sounded terrified. Maybe they were trapped, their coach overturned. Maybe Old Mom was hurt. Max sat up and slowly got to his feet.

Jodi ran through the pelting rain, mud clinging to her shoes. The train had folded up on itself, the cars a giant zigzag. People were standing in forlorn little groups or walking along the cars, obviously trying to find friends and family. Some of them carried lanterns, and Jodi saw a yellow glow lighting the windows of some of the cars that had remained upright.

"Have you seen Viktor?" Jodi asked a woman she recognized as one of the equestriennes.

"No. Have you seen my husband?"

Jodi shook her head. She knew the man only slightly. He was tall with a drooping mustache. The woman moved past her, scanning the faces

of a group standing beside one of the overturned cars. In front of them someone had set
down a lantern, and they had gathered around
it like people around a hearth.

Jodi veered toward them. She could hear the
rain sizzling on the slopped metal lantern top.
"Have you seen Viktor?"

"The Auguste? Is someone hurt?" one of the
men asked.

Jodi nodded. "My aunt needs a doctor."

"A lot of us do," one of the women said
bitterly. "They should hire a doctor to travel
with us."

Jodi did not recognize her in the dim light.
She was probably one of the generally useful
actresses who appeared in a number of acts and
the parade. Her right arm had been wrapped
with a crude bandage.

"We're going to stand out here all night, I
know," the woman said. "Half of us will probably get pneumonia."

Jodi glanced around. The darkness was teeming
with people who had no shelter. Only a few of
the cars stood upright at this end of the train,

and most of those were loaded with supplies and equipment. Jodi backed away from the lantern, slipping in the mud. No one said anything as she left. They were all staring off in different directions.

The next car up the line was upright, and Jodi climbed up the steps and leaned inside the open door. Ten or twelve people had crammed themselves into the first compartment, some on the bunks, some on the floor.

There was an enormously heavy woman with red hair. Jodi couldn't think of her name. She worked in the sideshow. Beside her, Fred Harris was doubled into a near ball, his long legs cramped under his chin. Two lanterns had been lit, and the air was acrid with the stench of coal oil in spite of the cold air and spattering rain coming in through the broken windows. "Has anyone here seen Viktor?" Jodi asked loudly.

"He was up by the menagerie wagons a while ago," Fred answered. His odd pinkish eyes glittered in the lantern light. "He was tending to the animal man."

"Mr. Grayson is hurt?"

The man shook his head. "No, but I think he's one of the ones trapped in a coach up there. I meant Cooper. Cooper is as sick as a dog. He collapsed trying to recage a cat."

Jodi nodded her thanks and ducked out of the car. She jumped down the steps. The rain was coming harder. Aunt Sophia had been chilled through and was probably shaking with cold.

As she passed the first of the menagerie cars, Jodi wondered if any of the animals had been hurt. The elephants were still trumpeting frantically as she went by their boxcar. It sat canted at a slight angle, and Jodi pitied the terrified animals chained inside. If Mr. Grayson was trapped and Mr. Cooper was too sick to help, there was a good chance a lot of the animals would end up hurting themselves in their panic. Where was Max? Jodi wondered. He would help Old Mom if he could. Next to Mr. Cooper, that elephant was his closest friend in the world.

Jodi ran past the elephant coach, trying to spot any movement in the dark, or to see a lantern lit. If Viktor was still with Mr. Cooper, it was probably up here somewhere. The next car held a lantern, but when Jodi climbed the steps and looked in, she only startled two men from the Wild West act who were trying to put their scattered belongings back in their trunks. She climbed down and went on.

Even once she was past the elephant coach, the trumpeting was so loud that it took a few seconds for her to realize that a high squeal of rending metal had joined the cacophony. She stumbled to a stop, turning, peering into the darkness. It was only the trembling of the ground that saved her life.

Startled by the strange vibration beneath her feet, Jodi backed up, looking down the track. A flash of white tusk passing the lantern-lit window sent her scrambling backward just in time to get out of the way.

The elephants had torn loose from the chains that held them inside their boxcar. As they stampeded past, shaking the ground, Jodi shrank against the side of an overturned coach car. One of the elephants bumped the car rounding the corner, and Jodi felt the tons of steel shift a few inches, shoving her forward.

A few seconds passed, and the vibration faded. Jodi held up one hand to keep the rain out of her eyes and hurried onward. Between two of the coaches, she saw a dark, hulking shape and realized that all of the elephants had not stampeded. Without Mr. Grayson or Mr. Cooper to supervise things, a lot of the animals might wind up in trouble. Jodi glanced back. The elephant had moved out of sight.

Jodi passed two more groups of people standing forlornly around hissing lanterns, their clothes soaked, their hair plastered to their foreheads. She stopped and asked if they were all right. No one she knew was too badly hurt. But no one had seen Viktor.

Jodi kept going, even though the front of the train held mostly damaged parade wagons and equipment bundled in soaked canvas. Jodi was about to give up and start back when she saw a single lantern up ahead. She caught a glimpse of a tall, rangy figure and shouted out as she broke into a run. "Viktor?"

"Yes?" He turned and squinted.

She knew he would be unable to see anything

beyond the circle of yellowish light. "Viktor, it's me, Jodi," she called breathlessly, pounding to a halt. "Aunt Sophia is hurt and—"

Viktor took her shoulders and held her steady. Only then did she see that she had nearly stumbled over Mr. Cooper, lying wrapped in wet blankets on top of what looked like a compartment door.

"I am glad to see you," Viktor said. "No one else has come up this far, and I need help, too."

Jodi nodded, her heart still thudding. "I'll do anything, but you have to go see to Aunt Sophia right away and—"

"You are a strong girl?" Viktor interrupted with maddening calm.

Jodi nodded again.

"Take his feet." Viktor motioned at Mr. Cooper's still form. Jodi bent low, pushing the blankets out of her way as she got a good grip on the edge of the door.

"Ready?" Viktor asked.

Jodi tested her grip. "Yes."

Together they lifted the door and started slowly through the mud.

CHAPTER TEN

Max's legs felt like rubber as he walked the narrow edge of the trestle, steadying himself with one hand on the skewed flatcars. It was raining hard. His feet were bleeding, but he was so cold, they didn't hurt yet.

Max could feel the pounding of the heavy wagons against the trestle's lowest timbers. The engine and several cars had plunged into the dark water. The calliope and the ticket wagon were gone—and some of the wagon cars. Max shivered.

A grating roar startled Max out of his thoughts. He walked carefully until he could make out a lion pacing anxiously inside its tilted cage. As he walked down the line of menagerie wagons still strapped to their flatcars, Max peered upward into the cages he passed. The rhinoceros lay sideways, its bony hip pressed into the bars. Its head was up and its eyes did not look dull, but Max couldn't tell if it was hurt. The cats he could see were miserable, wet and surly. Some of the cages were badly damaged, and a few had been thrown off their flatcars completely.

The cars had slammed into each other and lay angled in opposite directions, very nearly hanging over the edge of the trestle. Max had to duck under a coupling to get past the first flatcar, then he could step off the timbers and veer out across the meadow that bordered the tracks.

Max kept going, saying a silent prayer for Old Mom and the other elephants. He stared into the darkness ahead, hoping to see them at any second. Hickory would be uneasy and swaying. Donner and Norma probably would be looking for something to eat. Old Mom would have her ears spread wide to wash them in the rain.

The rushing of the water fell behind, lost in the sound of the rain. Then, with every step, Max began to hear other things. Horses were squealing and whinnying from every direction. People were shouting. He heard a violent pounding sound, like a canvas man's sledge-hammer beating against metal. There were two or three lanterns standing on the ground, and as he got closer, Max saw a group of ten or twelve men standing hunch-shouldered in the rain, all of them facing an overturned coach car.

"Mr. Grayson? Can you hear me?" someone shouted.

If there was an answer, Max couldn't make it out. The pounding started again. "Is Mr. Grayson all right?" Max called.

One of the men turned to peer at him. "Who's there? Max?"

Max recognized Mr. Smith. They shook hands, grinning.

"We thought you were long gone, boy," Mr. Smith said. He was cradling one arm, tied up in a piece of calico. Max smiled at him, happy that the older man had not been badly hurt.

"Grayson's in there." Mr. Smith jabbed a finger at the coach car. "It rolled onto the windows. The corridor collapsed."

"Is he—" Max began.

"He's all right," Mr. Smith said quickly. Then he chuckled. "But he's almost mad enough to chew his way out, I think. He'd better hurry. With Cooper down, he's the only who'll even try to go after the cats, I guarantee you that. I've got all the young men out chasing horses now."

Max turned and watched the roustabout slamming his sledgehammer into the sheet steel. There were a few pits and dents in the heavy metal, but no other sign of progress.

"Is Mr. Cooper hurt?" Max asked without taking his eyes off the roustabout.

"Viktor was up front somewhere tending to him, I was told. The wreck didn't hurt him, but he's got the cat-fever pretty bad. There's three out, you know, and the elephants."

"Out?"

Mr. Smith chuckled again, but this time he was shaking his head. "Poor cats. They hate this weather. They'll all end up under a coach somewhere trying to keep dry. You watch your step."

"Which way did the elephants go?" Max asked.

"Thataway," Mr. Smith answered, pointing. "And they're five miles away by now, son. But it's open country, all big ranches around here. They'll just graze a few trees to the ground and wait for someone to come get them."

Max nodded, taking a step back. "Nothing I can do to help here, is there?"

Mr. Smith shook his head. "I put two men up the track with lanterns to stop the morning train from running into us. Some others have gone off looking for a telephone, but I don't think there's one within fifty miles. These are all big wheat and corn spreads all through here."

Max nodded to show he had heard, but his mind was elsewhere. He wanted to find Mr. Cooper. Someone had to take charge of finding the animals.

Max let Mr. Smith show him the broken door of the elephant car, then they said good-bye and Max walked away, conscious that his feet were beginning to warm up a little. They ached.

The rain was a steady, pelting downpour now. As it went on, Max saw groups of people huddled against the train, trying to find at least a little shelter. Here and there he saw lanterns inside the upright cars and glimpsed silhouettes of people gathered around the light. He heard a gunshot, then a high whinny, and knew that Mr. Smith's crews were putting injured horses down now.

As Max plodded on through the mud, the heavy darkness of night was receding. In the east, the clouds were graying, but the stormy sky was holding back a real dawn. Max limped along, scanning the faces of people he passed. Those he recognized made small sounds of greeting, but no one stopped to talk.

When Max first came up behind the two people carrying the makeshift litter, he didn't recognize either one of them. Then Viktor's tall, lanky frame gave him away, and Max broke into a run to catch up.

"Viktor? Is that Mr. Cooper? Is he—"

"Max! I'm glad you are all right."

Jodi's voice startled him as he fell into step. He nodded at her, then looked anxiously at Mr. Cooper. His eyes were closed, and he was pale.

Viktor spoke over his shoulder without breaking stride. "We're taking him along so that I can keep an eye on him and Jodi's aunt at the same time."

Max dropped back. It was obvious that Jodi was straining to carry the weight. "I can take this end."

Jodi shot him a look of thanks as Viktor nodded and stopped. He waited while Max and Jodi carefully switched places. Then they went on.

Max stared down at Mr. Cooper. Even in the murky light it was obvious that he was really sick. There were dark circles underneath his eyes, and his cheeks looked hollow. Max struggled to keep up Viktor's long stride, grateful that the cold mud helped him ignore the pain in his feet.

"Hey, Viktor!"

Max turned to see a little boy come running out from the wrecked railroad cars. Jodi stopped to talk to him. Viktor slowed, then stopped, too.

Max looked back, bracing the metal door on his thigh.

"He's lost," Jodi called.

Viktor lifted his chin and spoke over his shoulder again. "John's mother is Elizabeth Hedge. She is with the sideshow. She's the big, red-haired woman. Do you know her, Jodi?"

"I saw your mother," Max heard Jodi tell the little boy. "I know where she is."

"Take John to her, then," Viktor said. "Then come back to your family. I'll see to Sophia."

"And keep an eye out for cats," Max warned Jodi. "Mr. Smith said some were out. And the elephants."

Jodi nodded. "I saw them stampede. But one stayed back. It might have been Old Mom."

Max felt his heart lift. "Was she all right?"

Jodi nodded, taking the boy's hand. "I think so. The others went toward the trestle, then veered off that way." She gestured toward the east.

Max smiled his thanks as Viktor led off, then glanced back once to see Jodi headed toward the front of the train, leading the little boy through the drizzle.

★ ★ ★

Everywhere along the side of the train, Jodi led John past groups of forlorn-looking people sitting or lying down in the mud.

"I'm cold," he said in a voice so low, she almost didn't hear him.

"Your mother is in one of the cars. It'll be warmer inside," Jodi answered, scanning the coaches as they passed. The truth was, she wasn't sure where she had seen Mrs. Hedge. Most of the cars were dark, empty. They were so full of twisted equipment or so dangerously tilted that no one could use them for shelter.

"My mother isn't hurt, is she? A lot of people are hurt."

Jodi held his hand tighter. "Your mother looked fine." She glanced up at the sky, blinking to keep the rain out of her eyes. It was getting light. It wouldn't be more than a few hours before help arrived, she was pretty sure. A swirl of wind kicked up and swept by, chilling her. John made a soft whimpering sound, but he didn't complain.

Finally, much farther up than she had

remembered, she found the right car. John started crying when he saw his mother, and she gave Jodi a smile of joyous relief.

"I couldn't find him afterward," she said through her tears. "His berth was empty, and the windows were all smashed. I looked outside, everywhere I could think of—"

Jodi nodded, feeling better as she went back down the slippery metal steps. At least one thing had gone the way it should.

The sky had brightened in the few minutes that Jodi had been inside. She could see the vague curve of the far side of the valley they were in, and the clumps of miserable people huddled alongside the back part of the train were more visible now, too.

Jodi squinted out across the countryside, hoping to see a lit window, somebody's warm kitchen, close enough to help. But there was no light in the gray valley. She pushed her hair back and felt cold rivulets run down inside her soaked shirt.

Jodi was about to turn and begin the long, cold wade through the mud back to Papa and the others. But then something caught her eye. In the grayish light of the stormy dawn, she saw a darker shape. Squinting, shielding her eyes from the falling rain, she began to smile. It was a barn, or maybe just a shed. It was hard to tell how far away it was, or how big. But if the roof was sound, it would serve to shelter at least some of the people until help arrived.

There was a distant rumble of thunder, the lightning too far away to help her see. But the rain began to fall harder. Glancing toward the rear of the train, she made a sudden decision. Viktor and Uncle Dominic and Papa would all see that Aunt Sophia got whatever care they could provide. And Viktor would take care of Papa's leg, too. Maybe it was almost as important to find shelter.

"Good-bye, Jodi," a high, happy voice called out, and Jodi turned to see John waving and smiling. She waved back. Then, imagining how happy everyone would be if she came back with the news that there was a warm, dry barn big enough to hold them all, she set out across the fields.

Jodi walked as fast as she could through the

mud and wet weeds. Halfway there, she stopped to roll up her trousers, shaking gobs of mud from the soaked cloth.

As she got closer, her hopes soared. It was a big building, probably the hay barn for some huge ranch. There was no sign of a house nearby, but she could see faint tracks leading away, the kind of wagon road that meant no one came here very often.

Jodi circled the building. It *was* a hay barn! There was a wide set of double doors barred from outside. Next to them was a smaller door, swinging open in the wind, its lift-latch rattling. Jodi slipped though it and stood just inside. It felt wonderful to be out of the rain.

She opened her jacket and pushed the tail of her damp nightgown beneath the waistband of her trousers. There were splatters of mud everywhere on her clothing. Her hair felt dirty and it clung to her scalp. Maybe somewhere on the train they could find dry towels and bedding. With everyone helping, they could carry enough inside a tarpaulin or tent canvas for the hurt people, at least.

Overhead, Jodi heard the thrumming of the rain get louder. She stepped away from the door, peering into the dark, cavernous barn. There were windows up high in the farthest wall. Was there a loft? If there was, everyone would be able to have a dry place to rest.

Jodi took a tentative step, afraid of walking into broken floorboards or some old rusty harrow. She blinked, then squeezed her eyes shut and counted to twenty. When she opened them, she could see a little better.

The barn appeared to be pretty much empty. Jodi stood still and turned in a slow circle. There were dark shapes stacked against the far wall. Probably just a few remaining piles of hay. She smiled. If it wasn't moldy, people could use it to make mattresses.

Jodi's eyes were adjusting to the darkness now. Overhead, down by the dirty windows, she could make out beams that crisscrossed the high ceiling. So there wasn't a loft, or at least it didn't extend the length of the building. Jodi walked carefully on the dusty floor, glancing upward as she went. There. Something solid obscured the beams. It was a half-loft. She grinned to herself. This was perfect.

The door suddenly slammed shut in the wind, the planks banging like a gunshot as the lift-latch caught and closed with a little metallic click. Jodi spun, instinctively looking for another way out. There wasn't one. Furious with herself, she started back toward the door, then stopped, her heart pounding. From the darkness ahead of her came the low, menacing growl of a big cat.

CHAPTER ELEVEN

Max stood off to one side. Viktor was talking in a low voice to Jodi's aunt. Her eyes were closed, but Max could hear her responding, her voice breathy and vague. Viktor had sent Jodi's uncle off to find clean water and something for bandages. Her father was sitting in the mud, his head resting on his knees, silent. For the first time, Max allowed himself to feel the pain and weariness in his own body. He exhaled, a long sigh.

Viktor looked up. "Are you all right?"

Max nodded. "But if you don't need me, I'd like to try to find Old Mom."

Viktor smiled. "Try to find some shoes, too. Then we can wash and bandage your feet."

Max looked down. The mud was so deep that his toes were covered. How had Viktor even noticed the blood?

"If you see Jodi coming back this way," Viktor went on, "tell her that I think her aunt will be fine after some rest."

The rain came down harder, the wind picking up a little. Max shivered. "I'll tell her, but you'll probably see her before I do." Nodding, Viktor turned away.

Max walked slowly. His feet ached in spite of the chilly mud. He lifted his head. It was getting lighter, at least. He couldn't see far through the rain, but he made out a line of trees that angled off to the west.

Picking his way through the weary and confused people who surrounded the wreck, Max walked the length of the train. He zigzagged, looking between the cars, stopping at the edge of the trestle. Old Mom was nowhere close. He crossed the tracks and headed for the tree line.

The deep mud gave way to more solid ground as Max followed the upward slope of the land, wincing as he stepped on grass stems and small rocks. Now that the early light allowed him to see it, the countryside was pretty, a gentle valley.

Glancing back, Max was astonished to see how small the wreck seemed in the wide meadows that surrounded it. He could see the knots of people huddled together, and for the first time, he noticed a picket line of horses near the caboose. Someone had been catching them up. Mr. Smith had probably organized it.

Walking on, Max noticed a wide swathe of flattened grass. Coming closer, he saw exactly what he had expected to see. There were huge, circular elephant tracks—some of them five or six inches deep in the wet earth.

Following the tracks, Max walked parallel to them, trying to spare his feet the sharp edges of the stones churned loose by the elephants' great weight. Watching his step, careful of the rocks, Max almost didn't look up in time to notice the single set of tracks leading from the train to a wide gully up ahead. Veering off, Max saw that this elephant's stride was shorter and fewer rocks had been dislodged. Max thought he knew the reason. This elephant had not been stampeding.

Following the single line of tracks, Max found himself skirting the line of trees for a while, then turning abruptly into them. Almost immediately, he heard the sound of rustling leaves and splintering wood.

Max walked cautiously toward the sound. After a moment, he spotted the gray, leathery skin of an elephant through the branches. A second after that, he saw Old Mom's huge head, her ears flapping to keep off the early morning mosquitoes. As Max stood, grinning, he saw her trunk snake upward, wrapping around a small limb. She broke it, then expertly stripped the leaves off, stuffing them in her mouth.

"Old Mom?"

She turned to face him, her jaw working. He watched as the last of the leaves disappeared into her mouth. She reached up for another branch and ate again, still staring at him.

"Will you go back with me?" Max asked her, knowing she would either let him lead her back because she liked him, or she wouldn't budge at all. He was pretty sure she wouldn't attack him—but not absolutely certain. She was a wild animal, and the train wreck had scared her.

"I can see why you wouldn't want to leave," Max said, walking a little closer. She stripped another branch of leaves, eyeing him as he approached. Her head was low, and her trunk was relaxed as she chewed. Max walked closer. If she let him touch her, she would probably respond to his cues. As he stepped under the canopy of the trees, the wind softened and he was protected from the worst of the rain.

"You found a good place," he said aloud.

Old Mom twitched an ear and swung her trunk upward, then down again. Max slicked his wet hair back from his face. It was a relief to be out of the rain. He leaned up against a tree trunk and resisted the urge to close his eyes and rest. "I'm so tired," he confided to Old Mom. "And my feet hurt bad."

He heard her ripping another branch mouthful of leaves from the tree, but he didn't open his eyes. This was probably as good as a holiday for the elephants, he thought—unless the others had gotten themselves into real trouble somehow. He had heard of elephants running amok, getting so frightened and angry that they killed someone they hated, or someone innocent by mistake.

Killer elephants almost always ended up being shot. No circus owner could afford to have an animal around that was dangerous to the audience. Old Mom shook, her leathery skin rustling, and Max opened his eyes.

"That will never happen to you," Max assured her, speaking aloud. "You are the gentlest elephant Mr. Cooper has ever worked with." Max smiled and nodded at her. "He told me so himself."

Old Mom suddenly extended her trunk to touch Max's face. He held very still as she brushed his cheek, then his ear, then laid her trunk along his neck in a friendly, trusting way.

"Will you let me take you back to the train now?" Max said. Then he hesitated. Why go back? It was wetter and colder up by the wreck than it was here. And here, Old Mom had fresh green leaves to eat—a treat for her. There was no guarantee at all that she would even respond to his commands. Max let her nuzzle him again and placed his hand loosely on her trunk.

"I don't want to take you back up there yet," Max admitted aloud. "Someone will make a picket line and they'll want me to chain you."

Old Mom swayed gently, then reached for another trunkful of leaves. Max watched. Were the other elephants as happy as Old Mom was right now? An idea began to form in his mind. If he brought the elephants back safe and sound, it would prove to Mr. Cooper that he could handle them—and that he was serious about learning to be an animal trainer.

"Mount," Max said.

Old Mom ignored him, reaching up for more leaves, her jaw working rhythmically.

Max cleared his throat. "Mount, Old Mom," he said again. This time, she swayed back and forth. He repeated the command once more, and she lowered her enormous weight, kneeling.

Feeling giddy that the magnificent animal liked him enough to do his bidding, Max stepped carefully up onto her leg. Then, moving as lightly as he could, he rested his weight for an instant on her tusk, then scrambled up to sit just behind her ears, careful to keep his weight off her tender spine.

"Up," Max said, and the tree branches that had been far above his head were suddenly close enough to brush against his hair. He scooted forward. It'd be hard to stay on without a harness to hang on to.

For a moment, Max considered going back up to the train and trying to find the elephant equipment, but then he decided not to. They would want to chain Old Mom up and make him leave elephant hunting to more experienced hands.

Max rubbed Old Mom's rough skin with the flat of his hand. She swayed beneath him, waiting. Max knew it wouldn't be much longer before help came. Men with proper tools would get Mr. Grayson out soon enough. Then, he would take over.

"Forward," Max said firmly to Old Mom, and she started off, her first enormous stride nearly unseating him. Coming out of the trees,

Max could see the wide path of churned earth
that marked the passage of the other elephants.
He turned Old Mom toward it, and she walked
faster, seeming to sense his intent.

Jodi held very still, her heart banging against
her rib cage. Where was the cat? She turned her
head a fraction of an inch. The snarl had come
from somewhere to her right—in the direction
of the door.

Paralyzed with fear, Jodi stood rigidly. The
darkness inside the barn seemed to deepen—
the little windows high in the far wall dimmed,
and she realized that a bank of storm clouds was
drifting overhead.

Jodi listened for any whisper of movement, a
paw on the dirt floor, the rustle of hay. But
overhead, the rattle of the rain intensified, making it impossible to hear. Jodi felt a sheen of
cold sweat form on her forehead. As the seconds ticked past, her eyes began to sting, but she
was afraid to lift her hand to wipe her brow.

Jodi ached to move, to turn and try to judge
the distance between herself and the loft. Was

there a ladder? She angled her head and squinted. She could see dark shapes—nothing more. They could be piles of hay as she had thought at first, or stacked saddles or rolls of fencing wire.

A clanking sound galvanized her whole body. The tiger had bumped something in the dark. It was moving fast, without caution. She took three quick steps toward the loft and she heard another growl from behind her. Jodi faltered, then ran.

Her heart beating in her ears, she fumbled her way along the far wall, banging her shins on some kind of metal box, raking her fingers along the wood. There had to be a ladder. There was always a ladder. How else could the farmer get up to the loft?

Another growl set her nerves on thin edge, and she fought desperate tears. Had the growl been closer? She hated the rain drumming on the roof, the thick clouds that kept the sun from shining through. She couldn't hear, couldn't see.

Stumbling sideways over a barrel that rolled beneath her, Jodi scrambled back up, reaching out to feel the wall, groping desperately for the ladder that she knew had to be there. But it was not.

Outside, the rain increased again, and Jodi could hear the wind rising as she followed the wall, fighting her fear. No one would come looking for her. No one had any idea where she had gone. Her hands balled into involuntary fists, and she reached out to beat them against the planks, bruising her knuckles on the edge of a crosspiece. It took her a few seconds to realize that she had found the ladder. She climbed with shaking knees, tears of relief streaming down her cheek.

CHAPTER TWELVE

Max lowered his head and rounded his shoulders against the pelting rain. Old Mom did not seem to mind it. She had been moving fast the whole time, the grassy ground rolling past beneath her heavy tread. At first, he'd had to touch her, guiding her along. Then, she understood what he wanted, and he had not had to cue her at all as she followed the tracks.

The rhythm of Old Mom's gait threw Max from side to side. Her skin was wet and slippery, and he leaned forward to hold on, his arms along the sides of her neck. For a long time, he simply hung on, raising his head now and then to make sure that she was still following the swath of trampled ground. The short, stiff hairs on the top of her head prickled at his skin.

Max saw the farmhouse in the distance and began to pray that the tracks would veer away from it, but they did not. As he got closer, he could see knee-high corn on either side of the house. One of the fields had a flattened path running through it.

Max guided Old Mom away from the tracks, keeping her parallel to the field for two reasons. First, he did not want to do more damage to the farmer's crop than had already been done. Second, if the man was furious and half blinded from the rain, Max didn't want to risk getting shot at.

The farmhouse remained silent and still as Max urged Old Mom past it. Maybe the family had slept in because of the rain, Max thought. Maybe they had simply not yet come out to notice the huge, round footprints that had ruined part of their crop.

Keeping the tracks in sight, Max turned Old Mom onto a dirt lane that ran between two plank-fenced pastures. The one on the west side of the road was grass, but on the right were old, gnarled apple trees with thick trunks and drooping limbs.

Old Mom's wide, flat feet made a sucking sound in the mud. The rain had let up a little, and Max sat straighter. He began to hope that he would soon spot the elephants standing quietly in some open field. But then he saw a broken place in the white plank fence that bordered the apple trees.

Knowing what seven hungry elephants could do to an orchard, Max guided Old Mom through the gap and then stopped her to scan the orchard. He couldn't see anything at first. The trees right along the road were untouched. But then he heard screams.

His stomach tight, scared that someone was already hurt, Max turned Old Mom down into the rows of big, spreading apple trees. She passed between them, branches scraping at her sides, abruptly lifting her trunk to trumpet. There was a trumpet in answer.

Old Mom moved faster without any urging and burst out from between the next pair of trees, breaking a low limb in her hurry. Then she slowed, and Max narrowed his eyes against the rain, straining to see. The screams were coming from two terrified children who clung to the stripped upper branches of one of the apple trees. Beneath it, Hickory stormed and raged. As Old Mom carried him closer, Max saw that Hickory's chain still dragged from the metal cuff that circled his right foreleg—and it had tangled in the lowest branches of the tree.

Max could see the other elephants scattered nearby. Donner was eating, his big ears flapping as he stripped leaves and shoved them in his mouth. Trilby was just past him, butting her head against the trunk of a tree, shaking it violently.

"Hey, you!" Max lifted his eyes and saw a man braced in a high fork in the tree Trilby was battering. The man was red-faced and held a rifle in his right hand. "Get these damnable animals off my property or so help me God I'll shoot every one of them dead."

Max signaled Old Mom to stop, trying frantically to figure out what to do. Hickory and

Trilby were the only ones who hadn't calmed down. Max watched Hickory fighting the tangled chain for a few seconds, wishing the big animal would just manage to break it before the shaking of the tree hurt the kids trying to cling to its branches. If one of them fell now, while Hickory was enraged, he might react as he would toward an enemy dropping from above. His instincts would tell him to trample and kill.

Over the thrashing of leaves and the heavy tread of the elephants, Max heard the unmistakable sound of a rifle being cocked. The farmer was standing unsteadily with his legs braced against stout branches, sighting downward at Trilby.

"Don't do it, Mister!" Max shouted. "You can't kill an elephant with a rabbit gun like that. If you hurt her, you'll find out she can rip that tree right out the ground."

Reluctantly, the farmer unshouldered his gun. Max looked at Trilby. She seemed to be butting the tree halfheartedly now. Her eyes weren't as wild as Hickory's. Max tried to figure out how to get close enough to free the

chain. If he could, Hickory would probably set-
tle down, surrounded by the calmer animals.

"Do something to help my kids, boy," the
farmer demanded.

Max turned to look at him. "If I can get—"

"If?" the farmer spat. "If? What do you
mean *if?*"

Hickory trumpeted again, jerking the chain
hard enough to make the tree tremble. The
children screamed. "The only reason I haven't
shot the crazy one," the farmer shouted at Max,
"is because I am afraid I'll hit my children from
here."

"If you shoot at him, he will go crazy," Max
shouted back. "And he just might kill us all."
Max glanced at the farmer. "I'm going to free
his chain if I can. Then he'll move off, I think."

The farmer didn't answer, and Max signaled
Old Mom to ease forward slowly. She obeyed as
perfectly as she always did for the Grand Entry,
taking one step, pausing, then taking another.
The swing of her stride was easier to sit going
this slowly, and Max found that he could loosen
the painful grip of his legs on her neck.

Hickory wheeled around to try to face Old Mom. The chain jerked him back, and he struggled against it. Max could hear the groaning of the tortured tree trunk. He had to do something before it snapped and threw the children into even worse danger.

Hickory shrilled another whistling trumpet, shaking his massive head as Old Mom sidled toward him. Max kept up a steady stream of compliments, telling her that she was going to save the lives of people and elephants. Her ears twitched back and forth, and he knew she was listening. She shouldered in close to the young bull.

Max bent his knees, keeping his legs high as Hickory slammed into Old Mom, nearly jolting Max off her broad neck. She grunted and swayed but held her ground. Hickory leaned into her again, shaking his head, his tusks dangerously close.

"Hang on hard," Max shouted up at the pale-faced kids. It was a boy and a girl. Neither one of them looked older than ten. "Don't come out of that tree until I tell you to," Max shouted. They both nodded solemnly.

Max gave Old Mom the command to step sideways. Leaning into Hickory, shoving him along with her, she obeyed. Max waited while Hickory fought the chain again, shaking the tree hard. The children wrapped their arms around a limb and closed their eyes.

"Once more," Max said to Old Mom. "Step left." She leaned hard into Hickory before she lifted her giant legs. Hickory trumpeted, and his trunk writhed, but he did not strike out.

Max could hear the farmer shouting, but couldn't understand what he was saying. It didn't matter. The only thing that was important was Old Mom's solid calmness. Max could see the chain clearly now. It had wrapped around a limb, and Hickory's frantic pulling had worked the metal links down into the soft wood. The end still dangled free. Max scanned the branches above his head, tracing a route down with his eyes. He could do it. And he would simply have to.

"Don't move," Max warned the kids again as he waited for Hickory to stop shoving against Old Mom. The moment she steadied, he got to his feet and took one shaky step along her back, careful to keep his weight off her spine. He gripped the branch closest to his head and pulled himself up onto it. Then, he started down, talking to Old Mom every inch of the way, pleading with her to keep Hickory away from him.

Finally, Max dropped to the ground, nearly crying out when his raw, sore feet struck the hard earth. He was on the far side of the tree from Hickory, and Old Mom stood between them. Still, it took all of his nerve to straddle the low limb, glancing up at Hickory's swaying form every few seconds.

The chain was so embedded in the tree that Max strained, gritting his teeth, pulling as hard as he could. It would not budge. He leaned forward, letting his arms go slack, breathing hard, his eyes fixed on Hickory. Then he tried again, jerking upward in sharp, sudden pulls that worked the first link free, then the second.

Max's breath was rapid and harsh with fear and effort. Every time Hickory pulled back, Max turned his head, afraid that the heavy chain would jerk loose and hit him. Timing the last few links with a moment's stillness, Max managed to drop the chain onto the grass, then scrambled upward just as Hickory tested the chain's fastness once more. It rattled over the ground, sliding without resistance. Hickory backed up several steps, his head low.

"Stand," Max said to Old Mom. "Stand. Stay with me." Then he looked at the kids. The girl's cheeks were streaming with tears. "Don't move yet," he told them, and pulled himself back up through the branches to slide onto Old Mom's neck.

Guiding her backward, he eased her alongside Hickory again, then sat perfectly still, opening his mouth so that even his breathing was silent. The farmer shouted, and Max turned to glare at him, then saw what the man was trying to tell him. Trilby had backed away from the tree and was looking toward Old Mom and Hickory. She took a hesitant step, then paused. After a few seconds, she took another.

"Everyone stay where you are," Max said, just loudly enough for his voice to carry. The moments ticked past, and Donner came to join the group of elephants around Old Mom. Max murmured praise as the others stopped their feeding and came close. Only once Hickory's anxious swaying had stopped did Max dare to utter the command: "Tail up."

Donner responded immediately, sidling back behind Old Mom. Norma came closer, and Big Girl and Donner sidled back and forth, sorting themselves out. There was some shuffling as they straightened out their line. "Tail up," Max repeated firmly as they positioned themselves.

Hickory hesitated, but Trilby stepped into place behind him and took his tail firmly in her trunk. Then, Hickory came forward and closed the gap in the line, Trilby following docilely. Max exhaled and allowed himself to smile as he turned toward the farmer and his children. "Sir, you can contact the Hamilton-Shaw Railroad Circus to pay for damages, but all three of you, stay up in those trees until we are gone."

"Thank you, Mister," the little girl called out as Max gave the command. He waved at her as Old Mom started off, leading the others out of the apple trees and back onto the muddy lane. Max followed the little road down the hill, then skirted the cornfield and picked up the stampede tracks on the far side.

Max's legs ached from gripping Old Mom's broad neck as the elephants traveled steadily across the countryside. The clouds broke up overhead and the sun came out just as Max came over the last rise and started down the slope toward the wrecked train.

Max exhaled in relief. Another train was stopped farther down the track—help had come at last. As he got closer, Max heard a shout and saw men pointing at him. A minute later, Mr. Grayson was riding a dapple-gray gelding toward him at a gallop.

"Max! We've been trying to find you!" he shouted as he reined in. "Mr. Cooper is going to be in your debt, young man." He gestured at the elephants.

Max smiled. "They finally got you out of the wreck."

Mr. Grayson nodded. "The pounding nearly deafened me, but the men finally broke through the steel. The worst is the horses. More than twenty were killed, and we've had to shoot others."

Max shivered, remembering the gunshot he had heard. "There's a farmer I think will be calling on the boss."

Mr. Grayson's face clouded. "Anyone hurt?"

Max shook his head, then explained what had happened.

Mr. Grayson smiled. "You've done a man's job today, Max. You should be proud of yourself."

Max stretched his legs out to relieve the ache.

"I'll take Old Mom on in," Mr. Grayson said. He dismounted and held out the reins. "Have Viktor look at your feet."

Max gave Old Mom the command, and she knelt so he could get off. Hidden by her bulk, he leaned forward, kissing her leathery skin. She blinked and lifted her trunk to touch his cheek.

Max's feet felt hot and swollen as he limped over to take the horse's reins from Mr. Grayson. Mr. Grayson approached Old Mom quietly, letting her smell him. Max mounted, then held the horse in as the elephants moved off. He followed, riding slowly.

There was a changed atmosphere along the train. People were moving with purpose now and even though they looked bedraggled and exhausted, they were smiling and talking.

"Max?" He reined in and turned in the saddle to see Mr. Jamison. "Have you see Jodi?"

Max shook his head. "Not since she left Viktor and me."

"Will you do me a favor?" Mr. Jamison asked. "My leg is pretty bad. Would you find her? Tell her Dominic has Sophia settled on the rescue train. They're taking out the sick and injured first, then coming back for the rest of us."

"Sure, Mr. Jamison," Max said. He turned his mount back toward the trestle. The first few people he encountered had not seen Jodi. Then, riding past a mosaic of blankets laid out to dry in the sun, he recognized the boy Jodi had helped.

"Have you seen Jodi Jamison?" Max called once he had managed to catch the boy's eye.

The boy raised his right hand to indicate the meadow on the opposite side of the train. "She walked off that way."

Max nodded his thanks and rode close to the coaches, finding a place where a coupling had broken, leaving enough of a gap for the horse to fit through. On the other side, Max scanned the countryside and saw what looked like a barn. He turned the horse toward it, wondering.

CHAPTER THIRTEEN

J odi had climbed the ladder in a panic, expecting the slash of claws across her back. But the cat had stayed on the ground. For a long time, she had been able to hear it pacing in the dark, its tail lashing in fury. It had been silent for a while, then had begun snarling again. Finally, it had come back to the ladder.

Jodi could not stop herself from trembling as she stood at the edge of the loft, listening to the cat below her. She could hear it sniffing at the ladder rungs, mouthing the wood. Was it hungry? The idea sickened her. People said that cats in cages were by far more dangerous than cats that lived wild. They weren't afraid of people anymore—they hated them.

The cat left the ladder to pace again, and Jodi sank gratefully to the floor of the loft, her legs weak with fear. There was no way out from up here. On the far side of the building, she could see the row of dusty windows . . . but there was no way to reach them.

The cat came back to the ladder, and Jodi scrambled to her feet at the sound of its claws digging at the wood. Then she heard a creaking sound as it began to climb, tearing at the planks and the ladder rungs as it struggled upward.

At first, Jodi could only press against the back wall of the loft, her heart pounding, her thoughts spinning in terrified circles. There had to be a way out. Maybe she could jump down out of the loft just as the cat leaped up. The idea dissolved as she pictured the cat turning gracefully to leap back down after her. The windows across the barn caught her eye, and she squinted at the maze of ceiling beams above her head.

For a few seconds she ran blindly around the walls, looking vainly for some way to climb higher. Finally, just as the cat scrabbled onto the edge of the loft floor, Jodi found long iron nails driven into the wall planks—probably to hang harnesses or tools.

Her hands and feet clumsy with fear, Jodi climbed the nails like an uneven ladder and dragged herself onto one of the beams. Below, the cat leaped upward, then fell back heavily. The beam was too high. Lying on the narrow rafter, Jodi watched the cat pace, snarling its frustration.

The sky brightened, and Jodi saw the cat clearly for the first time. It was the young Bengal that had attacked Mr. Cooper. Stories about man-eating tigers came unbidden into her mind. She tried to push them away, to tell herself that help would come—but there was no reason for anyone to come looking for her here, and she knew it.

It took the Bengal a long time to pull one of the planks free. Beneath it were three of the unpeeled poles that supported the walls. The Bengal sniffed the rough bark, curling its lip delicately. This kind of wood, it understood. It began to climb.

Jodi watched, horrified, standing up, ignoring

her cramped muscles as she turned and began to walk the beam. She stepped through the first of the V-shaped trusses, then glanced back. The cat was standing hesitantly on the first beam.

Jodi forced herself to keep going, but then, in the center of the cavernous barn, the sky overhead cleared and for the first time, bright sunlight streamed through the windows, casting rectangular patches of gold light on the floor twenty feet below. Jodi froze. Glancing back over her shoulder, she saw the cat coming toward her. It snarled.

Jodi looked down at the floor. It swam in her vision, and she realized that she had started to cry. She couldn't walk the beams any more than she could walk the high wire. The cat would get to her, or she would fall trying to get away from it.

"Jodi? Are you in there?"

She recognized Max's voice and tried to answer as the door banged open. She saw him standing silhouetted in the doorway, then she heard him gasp softly as he spotted her and the tiger.

"Walk on across," he said quietly. She could see him scanning the walls of the barn, then glancing back toward the door.

"I can't," she whispered.

He stared up at her. "You have to. I don't have a whip and even if I did, I can't control that cat. Mr. Cooper couldn't."

Jodi took a step, her arms out for balance. She wobbled and sank to a squatting position, her hand sweaty.

"You can do it," Max said.

Jodi glanced back at the tiger. It was watching them both, standing up again now. It snarled, low in its throat.

"Jodi!" Max whispered. "I'll find a way up on the outside and break a window to get you out."

He turned and ran, slamming the door behind himself. Jodi looked at it longingly, then glanced at the cat. It was coming toward her again.

A sudden thudding on the roof overhead made the cat stop and look up. Praying, remembering her mother's courage, Jodi stood up

straight and began to walk. The beams were narrow and they were rough, the splinters snagging
at her shoes. Jodi placed her feet carefully, keeping her eyes on the windows ahead, refusing to
look back at the tiger, or down at the hard floor
so far below. There was no net. It was up to her.

When Max's face appeared in the dusty glass,
Jodi felt herself steady a little. Staring at him,
glancing down at the beams only when she had
to step through the V-shaped braces, she made
her way toward him. He was motioning at her,
his mouth moving with encouraging words
that she could not hear. He shaded his eyes,
peering in as she got close, and she saw a look
of horror pass across his face.

The sudden snarl was so close behind her
that she trembled and froze again, glancing
back. The cat had followed her almost step for
step. It bared its teeth and snarled. Terrified, Jodi
hesitated, staring at it.

The sound of shattering glass made the cat
draw backward. Jodi turned toward the windows. She could hear Max shouting at the cat
now, his voice low and harsh. She was dimly

aware that he was leaning inside the window, throwing pieces of shingles and bits of wood past her, trying to hit the Bengal in the face, trying anything he could think of to make it pause just long enough for her to escape. She began to walk again, her eyes fixed on Max.

The beams ended about four feet from the far wall. Jodi hesitated again, but Max reached toward her, holding out his hands like an aerialist ready to make a steady catch. She measured the jump, knowing she had no choice. Her legs seemed to steady and strengthen as she ran the few last steps on the beam and sprang toward him, her own hands outstretched.

Max caught her wrists and dragged her forward. The cat crouched on the last beam, furious and snarling, swiping its inch-long claws at the empty air. Jodi began to cry, but Max was laughing as he set her back on her feet. He grinned giddily at her as he led her, limping, along the edge of the roof. His feet, she realized, were badly cut, but he slid down the rain spout he had climbed up, then helped her. Mr. Grayson's dapple-gray was tethered close by.

Max boosted her onto the horse. As they rode, he told her about Old Mom and the elephants.

"That's wonderful," Jodi said. "Mr. Cooper will have to start teaching you now."

Max looked back over his shoulder. "You think so?"

She nodded, smiling at his eager expression. "And I don't think I will be as afraid on the high wire anymore," she said. "Thank you, Max. If you hadn't come . . ." Max was facing front again and he didn't turn or interrupt her as she struggled with her thoughts. "The Bengal would have gotten me, Max. I would never have walked that beam without you there."

"You can pay me back someday," he said quietly. "Everybody in the circus needs help sometime."

"I will," Jodi promised.

"I could never walk the wire like you do," Max added. "I'd fall every time."

"The cats scare me," Jodi told him. "I can't imagine getting into that little cage with them."

"Sometimes, I can't, either," Max admitted.

"But I am going to do it. I think." He turned so she could see him smile.

Jodi grinned back at him. "If I can help you, I will."

Max nodded. Then, without warning, he dug his heels into the horse's sides, and they galloped toward the train.

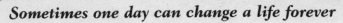

Sometimes one day can change a life forever

American Diaries

Different girls,
living in different periods of America's past
reveal their hearts' secrets in the pages
of their diaries. Each one faces a challenge
that will change her life forever.
Don't miss any of their stories:

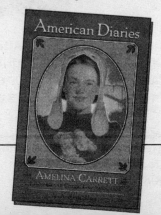